Cathy Cassidy

SAMI'S SILVER LINING

PUFFIN

PUFFIN BOOKS

UK | USA | Canada | Ireland | Australia
India | New Zealand | South Africa

Puffin Books is part of the Penguin Random House group of companies
whose addresses can be found at global.penguinrandomhouse.com.

www.penguin.co.uk
www.puffin.co.uk
www.ladybird.co.uk

First published 2018
This edition published 2019
001

Set in 12.32/17.9 pt Baskerville MT Std
Typeset by Jouve (UK), Milton Keynes
Printed and bound in Great Britain by Clays Ltd, Elcograf S.p.A.

A CIP catalogue record for this book is available from the British Library

ISBN: 978–0–241–33448–5

All correspondence to:
Puffin Books
Penguin Random House Children's
80 Strand, London WC2R 0RL

Thanks . . .

Thanks as always to Liam, Cal, Cait and all of my fab family.
Hugs to Helen, Fiona, Lal, Mel, Sheena, Jessie, Kicki and all of my
lovely friends near and far. Thanks to Annie, who arranges my
tours, Martyn who sorts out the number stuff and my agent Darley
and his team. Thank you to Erin for the cool artwork; to my editor
Carmen; and to Wendy, Mary-Jane, Tania, Roz, Ellen, Becca,
Lucie and all of the Puffin team for their help and support.

A special thank-you to the support staff and clients at SWAP in
Wigan, especially Basel and Rose for sharing their stories and their
food with me; to Sally from CRIBS International; and to Malena,
Ana, Rory, Jan and Jackie for caring – and – helping so much. Thanks
to Jen for ongoing musical advice, Tom for the hip hop info, and Cait for
the lyrics of 'Song for the Sea' and 'Setting Sun'. Thank you once more to
Mary Shelley the tortoise, for lending her name!

Most of all, thanks to YOU, my lovely readers, for being so
awesome and cool, and for making all the hard work worthwhile.

Cathy Cassidy, x x x

The sun rises slowly over the island in a blur of red and gold – I think it will be the last thing I ever see.

My breathing is raw, ragged, and I'm struggling to keep my head above the crashing waves. I think that I have swallowed half the Aegean Sea, that I might as well stop fighting, give in to it, let myself sink down beneath the surface and die.

I am cold, so cold my limbs feel like ice, and the salt that crusts my lips feels like frost. The island looks closer now, but it might as well be a million miles away because I have no more fight left in me – I have nothing at all. Another

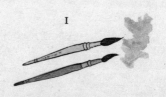

wave lifts me and carries me forward, leaving me face down in the shallows. My hands claw at wet, gritty sand, and I lie exhausted, frozen, gasping for air.

All is lost.

1

Lucky

They say I am lucky, the luckiest boy alive. They say that I must be brave and strong to have survived the hardships life has thrown at me, that I have been given a chance for a new beginning and must grab that chance with both hands.

I am lucky, lucky, lucky . . . or so they tell me.

I didn't choose any of this, and new beginnings feel empty and hollow when you have nobody to share them with.

Well, I have my aunt, my uncle and two grown-up cousins I've barely met. But although they have opened their arms and their hearts to me, I cannot do the same. I cannot let myself care any more, because I am not as strong as people think. I am broken, useless, like a piece of damaged pottery

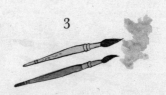

that looks whole but can never be the same again. I look OK on the outside, but inside I am flawed, fractured.

I am not what people think.

I am a fifteen-year-old boy held together with glue and good luck. There will come a time when my luck runs out, and I will fall apart. The world will see that I was damaged and hurting all along, and perhaps people will understand me a little better. Of course, it will be too late by then.

Sometimes I wish that we had never left Syria, even though our city was a war zone, and everyone an enemy. The government my father and mother once respected had turned against the people, and rebels took to the streets to fight back. Then came the extremists, like vultures feeding on carrion, bringing harsh new laws that dragged us all back to the dark ages. We prayed for the west to help us, but when help arrived it came in the form of western bombs that rained down from the skies and destroyed what was left of the place I once called home.

Sometimes I wish that we had stayed in the refugee camp, even though we were crammed three families to a tent, each tent so close they were almost touching. So close that sickness spread faster than wildfire.

I wish we hadn't taken passage on that boat to Kos, but my father said it would be one step closer to Britain, where my mother's brother lived. Uncle Dara and Aunt Zenna would give us shelter. Sometimes I wish I had stopped fighting then and sunk beneath the waves of the Aegean Sea, the way my father, my mother and my sister did.

I was the lucky one.

I swallowed down my grief, carried it inside me, but it was like a parasite that gnawed away at everything that was good. Eventually I got to the mainland and joined a long line of people who were walking across Europe. I walked until the soles of my boots were worn away, until I had gathered a group of kids around me, who like me were travelling alone. We stuck together because it was safer that way, but still we faced danger every day. We grew tough and cynical and ruthless, and we cried silently at night for all that we had lost. At a camp on the Italian border, charity workers tried to find us places to live. I told them I had family in Britain, and after a long wait they managed to trace my uncle and aunt and get me added to the last consignment of unaccompanied refugee minors to be allowed into the UK.

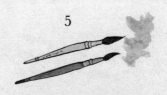

All I knew of my aunt and uncle were the stories my parents had told and a vague idea that they ran a tailor's shop in London. In fact, they didn't live in London at all, and the tailor's shop was actually a dry-cleaner's, but the charity that was helping me back then tracked them down anyway.

I remember the first time I saw Uncle Dara and Aunt Zenna, standing on the pavement outside the shop to welcome me, the nephew they hadn't even known they had. They were older than my parents, but Dara had a look of my mother all the same: dark wavy hair, stern brows, eyes that glinted with the promise of mischief.

'My little sister Yasmine's boy!' my uncle said, anguished. 'After all this time, how can it be? You are welcome here, Sami. We are family, yes?' He threw his arms around me and I felt the dampness of his tears against my cheek.

I was safe.

I was lucky.

I was home.

My father liked to look at the stars. He would sit on the flat roof of our old house in Damascus, where the railings were lined with terracotta pots of tomatoes, aubergines and peppers, and the warm breeze was heavy with the scent of jasmine, and we'd gaze at the big dark canopy of the night sky.

'Play the flute for us, Sami,' my father would say, and I'd work my way through my scales yet again, squeaky and slow. I got better, of course, until I could play pretty well, until I could provide a soundtrack for my father to look at the stars.

'Head in the clouds,' my mother would say, but there were rarely any clouds back then — just acres of sky, cool as silk, pierced with little bursts of silver light.

My father loved the night sky so much that he moved the old brass bedstead up to the roof. He and my mother slept there, while my little sister Roza and I would lie on our narrow beds in the room below and listen to the whisper of their voices, faint and reassuring, like distant birdsong. If it rained, which was rare, my mother would grab the pillows and the coverlet, and run down into the house, and my father would grab the bedroll and follow her.

2

Lost & Found

I live in Millford now, a small town in the English Midlands. Uncle Dara and Aunt Zenna run a small shop that does dry-cleaning and alterations, with a workshop and a flat above. I sleep in the room that belonged to my cousin Taz before he left home to work in London. My cousin Faizah's old room lies empty; she is married with a little boy now, and lives in Birmingham. The third bedroom belongs to my aunt and uncle.

There is no roof garden and no warm breeze that smells of jasmine – just a fire escape, a rusting metal staircase with ancient, warped railings, bolted to the back of the building. It has a view of the skip behind the charity shop next door and the orange glow of street lights hides the stars, but still, I like to sit here, playing the flute or reading a library book. The fire escape rattles in the wind and shudders a little when you climb it, but it is still my favourite place in Millford.

School, by contrast, is my least favourite place.

I was always going to stick out, a tall, skinny kid with black hair like a bird's nest and a worn, threadbare tweed overcoat.

'Welcome to Millford Park Academy,' Mr Simpson, the head teacher, had said on my first day. 'We are pleased to have you, Samir. I hope that in time you will come to feel at home here.'

At home? Really? I forced a smile. 'Thank you,' I said.

The head teacher frowned. 'The overcoat will have to go, though,' he said. 'We have a strict uniform policy here, and that coat is . . . well, it's not part of our dress code.'

I shook my head. I was grateful to the head teacher for allowing me to continue my education after the nightmare of the past few years, but I was not willing to part with the coat. It had been with me for most of my journey across Europe; it meant more to me than I could ever put into words.

9

'The coat, I will keep,' I said slowly and carefully.

'I think perhaps I'd better speak to your social worker,' he said with a sigh. 'Go along to class now. We can sort out the coat issue later.'

My social worker, Ben, came into school and talked to Mr Simpson, and the 'coat issue' was sorted. No teacher ever asked me to take the coat off after that, not even in PE lessons. They raised an eyebrow occasionally, or frowned at the coat, or sighed in a long-suffering kind of way, but they never spoke of it again.

The kids at Millford Park were not as polite, of course.

'What's with the coat?' they asked.

'Bet it stinks! Look at it – filthy!'

'Looks like someone died in it.'

'Miss, Miss, how come Samir is allowed to wear his coat in class and I'm not allowed to wear my studded belt? 'S not fair!'

I kept my head down through it all. My English was OK, and getting better all the time, but it seemed safer to stay silent.

'Your teachers say you're not talking, not integrating,'

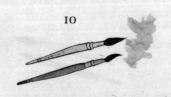

Mr Simpson said to me, a few weeks later. 'It must be hard for you, Samir, we understand that, but you must make an effort. You have to try.'

'Yes, sir,' I replied. 'I will try.'

The head teacher looked pleased. 'That's the spirit,' he said.

He meant well, but Mr Simpson had no idea what it felt like to be me. I was barely holding myself together back then, and making an effort to fit in was not high on my agenda. Besides, I don't think any amount of trying would have made much difference.

The kids in my year asked awkward questions. Most were just curious or concerned or kind, but some said things that were cruel and shocking, words so sharp that they made my head rage, my heart ache.

One day, a couple of months in, I was in the school lunch hall, half-heartedly picking at the packed lunch my Aunt Zenna had made for me. I'd chosen an empty table, but there were primary school kids visiting that day and they'd taken over three big tables, shrieking and laughing while their teachers looked on fondly. I tried to remember myself

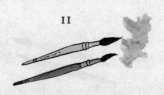

at that age, a bright-eyed kid without a care in the world, but I couldn't dredge up anything at all. The memories had gone, like smoke in the wind.

The lunch hall was full to bursting and a bunch of kids from my year were scanning the room for seats. They spotted me, alone in the corner, and swarmed around me, filling the table with plates of salty chips and pizza and salad, bowls of chocolate pudding and custard.

'All right, Sami,' one of the boys said, a kid from my English class who never went anywhere without a guitar slung across his back. Marley Hayes, his name was.

I nodded in acknowledgement, then dropped my eyes to the table again. I wondered how long I should wait before getting up and walking away, wondered what length of time would be enough to stop me seeming rude, impolite.

'Not that friendly, is he?' another boy said, a red-haired kid with a cold, hard stare.

'Probably doesn't understand English,' one of the girls chipped in. 'It's so sad, what he must have been through.'

'Sad?' the red-haired kid echoed, scowling at me. 'Don't be fooled. He can't be trusted – look at him, watching, waiting. I'm on to you, mate, OK? I know your game.'

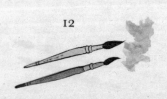

The hairs on the back of my neck prickled, and I pulled my chair back from the table, put the lid on my lunch box. Time to go.

'What *is* his game?' Marley asked the scowly kid, frowning. 'Why don't you tell me, Rory? What's he ever done to you?'

The boy sighed and shook his head. 'Obvious, innit?' he snarled. 'It's not what he's done – it's what he *might* do. He might be one of them extremist types.'

I flinched at the word, and he pushed his face right up against mine, so close I could smell cheese-and-onion crisps and bad breath and cruelty.

'Am I right?' he asked, so close that a fleck of warm spittle landed on my cheek. 'Are you a *terrorist*?'

I wished that I had no English, that I didn't understand, but I did. I understood all too well.

It seemed I would always be seen as an outsider, a threat, a danger, no matter how far that might be from the truth. I stood up, shaking, pulled my backpack on to one shoulder.

'What's up?' the boy spat. 'Got nothin' to say?'

I looked up, saw the hate in his eyes and wondered what I'd done to deserve it, wondered if he'd ever know how far off the mark he really was, or if he'd even care.

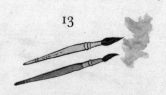

Then I saw Marley Hayes launch himself at the red-haired boy. A fist grazed his jaw with a crunching sound, then Marley grabbed his hair and pushed his face into a dish of chocolate pudding and custard.

'You're a loser, Rory,' Marley said. 'A nasty, twisted little loser. Seriously, you are.'

The school lunch hall was silent, dozens of primary kids wide-eyed at the spectacle. One little girl with pigtails burst into noisy tears, and a teacher leaned in to comfort her. Mr Simpson slammed through the double doors, stomping to a halt beside our table.

'You again, Hayes,' he snapped, glaring at Marley. 'Why am I not surprised?'

The red-headed kid wiped the custard from his face and he and Marley Hayes followed the head teacher from the hall.

That was the first time I had anything to do with Marley Hayes.

A few months later, I was playing my flute in the music room at school one lunchtime, alone and lost in the music. The flute was the one possession I'd carried all the way across

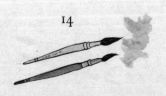

Europe, the one thing that hadn't been lost to the Aegean Sea. Its plastic case had protected it from the worst ravages of the salt water, and my aunt and uncle paid for it to be restored. Playing it was the one sure way of finding peace in the madness of a British secondary school, of keeping the past at bay. When I stopped, there was Marley Hayes, leaning in the doorway, doing a slow hand clap.

'Sami, you're actually a freakin' flute genius,' he said, one eyebrow raised. 'Who knew? Did you play back home in Syria?'

'A bit,' I said.

'I know a girl who's starting a band,' Marley said to me. 'They probably need a flute player. You in?'

'Um, dunno . . . maybe . . .'

It was the last thing I wanted to do, but Marley Hayes dragged me along to audition for a band called the Lost & Found. I must have passed the audition because suddenly I had something to do with my spare time, a place to go, people to hang out with. I had friends, sort of, and a chance to deaden the pain with music.

I have Marley Hayes to thank for all of that.

I used to like school, back in Damascus. The lessons were easy for me, and I loved to read, loved to paint, loved to play the flute. 'University material,' my father said proudly.

I had plenty of friends back then too. I didn't even think about it – when you're a kid, friendship is as easy as breathing. I used to play football with my best friend Azif and a whole gang of other boys, a rough-and-tumble tangle of arms and legs, of laughter and dust with the hot sun beating down on our heads.

One day the ball flew out of the playground and into the courtyard beyond, and I ran out to rescue it. It rolled to a halt beside the feet of a girl called Rania, who automatically reached out one sandalled foot and scooped the ball upwards, so that she could hand it back to me. I don't know if I fell for her football skills or her long-lashed brown eyes, her gap-toothed smile or the dark, rope-like plaits that reached to her waist – whatever it was, I was smitten.

Rania was my first crush – we were eight years old.

I heard that her family went to the camps in Jordan, when the fighting started. I never saw her again.

3

Someone Else's Girl

I guess you could say that the Lost & Found rescued me. Suddenly, I had a bunch of new friends and a chance to play the flute without worrying about whether it would annoy my aunt and uncle. I was part of something. Rehearsals were chaotic, as we worked out how to pull things together, find a style with our original songs. Marley provided a basic melody and a girl called Lexie Lawlor wrote the lyrics, and the rest of us worked out how to fit in around it all, mostly by trial and error.

There was a lot of error, to start with at any rate.

Sometimes, when I was waiting for my cue or hanging about while Marley coached the others, I'd take a little notebook from the pocket of the threadbare overcoat and draw. Ben the social worker had given me the book, with the idea that I could write down thoughts and memories in it, things that were too difficult or painful to say out loud. I did that sometimes, but other times I just drew, because it was easier and less upsetting, and the notebook had blank, creamy white pages that were just begging to be doodled on.

After a while I stopped worrying whether the kids in the band would think I was weird. The notebook was something to hide behind, something that helped me to make sense of my new band mates and maybe helped them to make sense of me.

The Lost & Found

Marley Hayes — lead guitar — determined to be famous!

Dylan Hayes — drums — Marley's little brother

Lexie Lawlor — backing vocals, lyrics

Bex Murray — bass guitar — Lexie's foster sister — kind of fierce

Lee Mackintosh — trumpet — a bit of a joker

George Clark — cello — smart, serious, wants to be a physicist

Happiness Akebe — violin — really clever, really talented, makes amazing cakes

Romy Thomas — violin and backing vocals — really quiet and shy

Sasha Kaminski — lead vocals — really pretty, amazing voice

Jake Cooke — triangle — well, that's a joke, really (Jake's what they call the roadie, the tech guy, I suppose)

Soumia Murad — ~~keyboards — bit stressed out with GCSEs just now~~

SOUMIA QUIT THE BAND, WE NEED A NEW KEYBOARDIST

And then there was me, the quiet kid with the tatty overcoat and the bird's-nest hair, the boy who hadn't had a crush since he was eight years old and a whole world away . . . until I met Lexie Lawlor.

I thought that my heart had turned to stone, but I guess it was actually ice, because when I met Lexie, the tiniest corner of my frozen feelings began to thaw. It was like one of those documentaries about the Arctic tundra when the ice starts to melt, one drip at a time. Something about Lexie got under my skin – when she was around, the world looked

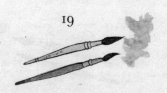

19

brighter, somehow. She wore her feelings on her sleeve, with a rawness, a vulnerability I'd never seen before.

Lexie was thirteen years old, with big, sad eyes that gazed out from beneath one of those shrunk-in-the-wash fringes. When she wasn't in school uniform she mooched about in little flippy skirts and T-shirts with cartoon characters or clever slogans on them. She couldn't have been more different from Rania, but every time I looked at her I felt my world slip sideways.

I was out of practice at feeling that way. Shyly handing over a boiled sweet might pass for true love when you're eight years old, but I was pretty sure that more would be required now.

No girl in her right mind would want to get involved with me, anyway. I was a mess – part iceberg, part human wreckage – but that wasn't my only problem. Marley and Lexie ran the Lost & Found between them, and together they wrote the kind of songs that made you shiver. They were a good team, but the teamwork didn't stop at songwriting. Lexie and Marley were dating – she was someone else's girl, and that someone else was supposed to be my friend.

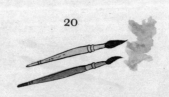

A little bit of my frozen heart died all over again once I worked that out, but it was too late by then. I'd fallen for Lexie, hard.

By then I'd worked out that Lexie and Bex weren't just friends but foster sisters.

'How come Lexie and Bex are in foster care?' I asked Marley, trying to be casual. It probably didn't seem all that casual, seeing as I was the kid who hardly ever spoke, but I wanted to know and Marley was the only one I felt I could ask.

'Bex's parents were a bit messed up and couldn't look after her,' Marley explained. 'As for Lexie . . . well, her mum went missing when she was nine years old. Nobody's ever found out what happened to her – Lexie was found alone in an empty flat, hungry and abandoned. So, yeah – she ended up in foster too.'

I just nodded, non-committal, but my iceberg heart was thumping.

Marley narrowed his eyes.

'You like her, don't you?' he wanted to know. 'Lexie. You have for a while.'

I said nothing, pretended I hadn't even heard. The skin

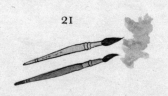

on my cheekbones burned a little, but if I stayed calm I was pretty sure that Marley would move on to a different topic. He didn't.

'You do know we're not together any more, don't you?' he told me. 'Me and Lexie. We split up a couple of weeks back. We're just friends now . . . Well, that's all we ever were, really. Just in case you didn't know. Just in case you do like her.'

I shrugged, as if it didn't matter to me one way or another, but my stomach flipped over. I learned a whole lot about Lexie that day.

I understood now why she had such sadness in her eyes, why she wrote the kind of lyrics that made you catch your breath. Lexie knew what it was like to be lost. Maybe a part of her heart was in the deep freeze too. Maybe she woke up in the darkness trembling, afraid, trapped in nightmares of the past. Maybe.

I understood then why I felt so drawn to Lexie, why out of all the girls I'd met since coming to Britain, she was the one I'd fallen for.

Lexie Lawlor was damaged, just like me.

WANTED

Dynamic new Millford band the Lost & Found are looking for a talented keyboard player aged 12–16 with the drive, energy and ambition to make it to the very top. We play our own original material, indie ballads with a sixties pop twist.

Must be available for daily rehearsals throughout the summer holidays, gigs, recording and more. No time-wasters.

For an audition slot and further details, email

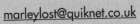

marleylost@quiknet.co.uk

4

Auditions

'Sami, isn't it time to stop wearing the coat?' Aunt Zenna says as I get ready to head out to the auditions. 'It's much too hot today – you'll melt! Perhaps it's time to think about putting it away, storing it safely before it falls apart at the seams?'

'I'll be fine, Aunt Zenna,' I reply, although I know she has a point.

My bird's-nest hair is still damp from the shower and falling around my face in snake-like strands and I'm wearing a clean black T-shirt and dark skinny jeans, but I know the coat probably cancels out any attempt to look cool. It really is falling apart – the cuffs are in shreds and the hem is frayed and faded, but I am not ready to let go of it just yet.

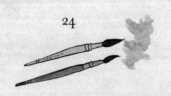

I'm not sure if I ever will be.

'Will you be in for tea?' Aunt Zenna asks. 'You said there was no band practice today, so I'm making chickpea stew with baklava for afters. Your favourite!'

'Thanks,' I say. 'No worries . . . I'll be here!'

My aunt and uncle are trying hard to help me settle in, but sometimes it feels like we are three strangers sharing a space. Sometimes I just want to shout and yell and slam doors, and sometimes I want to hide away from the world. Instead, I have to smile and make small talk and pretend that baklava is my favourite. I am doing my best, anyhow – I think we all are.

I sling my flute case over one shoulder and I'm out of there, pulling the door shut behind me, running down the stairs that lead past the workroom. As I pass the glass door that leads through to the dry-cleaning shop, I catch a glimpse of Uncle Dara, whistling as he fills out an order form for a wedding dress that has been brought in for alteration. I wave at him in passing and he stops whistling to smile, a big, joyful grin that reminds me so much of my mother that my eyes blur briefly, and I have to wipe one frayed sleeve across my face before I head out to the street.

*

25

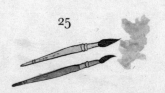

The posters have been up all over town for ten days now. They're on the wall in the Leaping Llama, the hipster cafe Marley likes to hang out at, and also a whole lot of other local cafes and shops. The music shop has given us pride of place on their noticeboard, and when I call into the newsagent on the corner to buy a fineliner pen for my drawings there's one on the door. It gives me a little buzz of pride to see my artwork in poster form, helping us in our quest to find a new keyboard player.

At the end of term, we played at a big music festival in the park to try to save five local libraries that had been threatened with closure. It was a great gig with loads of publicity, and it had turned the tide for the libraries, because the council changed their tune and decided that they could stay open after all. Sadly, the publicity backfired on us a bit. It turned out that Soumia, our keyboardist, had told her parents she'd quit the band to focus on her GCSEs. When they saw their daughter on the local TV news channel, on a floodlit stage, playing to a crowd of thousands, the cat was out of the bag.

Soumia's parents made her quit the band for real the next day. 'Exams come first,' she'd explained sadly. 'The

GCSEs are done, but it's A levels next. Mum and Dad don't think music is a proper career. Sorry.'

We were down a band member, and although Sasha, our lead singer, had been filling in for her, we really needed a proper replacement.

'Make us a poster, Sami?' Marley had said, and I had.

The auditions are being held this afternoon at the old railway carriage where we practise.

The practice space is an awesome vintage railway carriage in the grounds of a big mansion house called Greystones, which belongs to an eccentric elderly artist and ex model called Louisa Winter. Jake helped to arrange for us to use it – his family live in part of the house, along with a few other arty, alternative types, so it was just a case of asking Louisa Winter for permission.

As I walk across the grass towards the old railway carriage, I see Marley Hayes standing on the steps, drinking orange juice straight from the carton, with Dylan, Jake, Lexie, Bex and Happi lounging on the grass nearby.

'Hey, Sami!' Marley greets me. 'Let's hope we find someone today. We can't keep expecting Sasha to multitask, especially now that we're on the brink of stardom . . .'

27

'Stardom?' echoes Bex, whose hair has turned a startling shade of sea green since our last band practice. 'We're doing OK, Marley, but I think stardom might be pushing it just a little bit!'

'That's the difference between us, Bex,' Marley says. 'I have vision. You do not.'

'I have vision,' Bex argues. 'I just think we need a lot more practice, a lot more songs and some of that mentoring Ked Wilder offered us. It's a pity he's away in France all summer.'

Ked Wilder is a sixties pop legend, and a great friend of Louisa Winter. Ked headlined the music festival we were part of a few weeks back, and he'd liked our stuff so much he'd offered to help us get a foot on the ladder to success. The trouble is, he's been at his villa in France ever since, and although Marley Hayes is a boy of many talents, being patient is not one of them.

'I want to make sure we keep moving forward,' Marley says. 'With or without Ked Wilder. That's what this is about! We've had a few applicants, thanks to Sami's posters. I've made a shortlist, and the first candidate's due any minute, so I guess we should get going. The plan is to talk to them

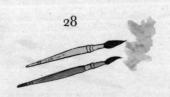

and let them play a piece, and then, if they're good enough, see how they go with one of our songs.'

Marley turns back into the railway carriage, the six of us trailing after him.

Two hours later, we are no nearer to finding our new band member. First comes Bernard, a classically trained pianist who plays some Beethoven for us but can't be a day over nine years old; then Sid, who taught himself to play by listening to Disney soundtracks and plays us a tear-jerking version of 'When You Wish Upon a Star', though he keeps stopping to nibble at the badly chipped black nail varnish on his bitten nails.

I start sketching the candidates in the back of my notebook while the others clown around with secret scoresheets and scribbled messages passed between them. So far, the highest score – a six – goes to Manda, who plays a passable version of 'Somewhere Over the Rainbow' and tells us all about the ballet, tap, jazz, voice and acting classes she has every night after school. On the way out she tells us she doesn't really have time for anything else and was just curious to see what the audition would be like.

Great.

Next comes Rick, a kid who got expelled from Millford Park Academy last year for hacking into the computer system and posting dodgy photoshopped pictures of his most hated teachers on the school website. He's in a band called Zombie Massacre but says he wants to go more mainstream, and has composed a complex heavy metal/techno-beat keyboard piece that goes on for forty minutes and almost makes my ears bleed. Marley smiles his most charming smile (in case Rick decides to take some warped online revenge) and says he'll be in touch.

'What a bunch of weirdos!' Dylan grumbles. 'Isn't there anyone . . . well, normal?'

'Why would someone normal want to get mixed up with us lot?' Bex asks, and Dylan shrugs and says it's a fair point.

Marley checks his watch. 'One more candidate,' he says. 'Guys, it's not looking good – and this was the shortlist. I'd already weeded out the really awful ones. What if we take Bernard and give him a big hat and make him stand on a box?'

'I know you're joking,' Bex says. 'I'm just not seeing the funny side right now.'

There's a sharp rap on the open door of the railway carriage, and the last candidate appears in the doorway.

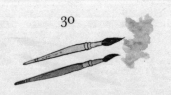

'Hi, guys,' she says, her fingers fluttering at us. 'I'm Bobbi-Jo Bright, and I am so excited to meet you! I watched you play at the festival in the park a couple of weeks back, and now . . . well, here I am!'

I've never seen Bobbi-Jo before, and one glance at the others tells me they don't know her either. She's the kind of girl you'd remember. She's wearing a lot of make-up and a retro style minidress with shiny black ankle boots – she looks cool and confident and a little bit bizarre, like she's just stepped off the set of a 1960s TV show.

'OK,' Marley says. 'Welcome, Bobbi-Jo! Can you tell us anything about yourself? Why are you interested in being our new keyboardist?'

Bobbi-Jo perches on a high stool in the middle of the railway carriage, just behind the borrowed keyboard that nobody bothered to take back to Millford Park Academy after Soumia's departure. She smiles, displaying very white teeth. It's an unsettling sort of smile – it reminds me of a small animal that might growl or bite at any moment.

Bobbi-Jo tells us that she lives in a village called Brookleigh, halfway between here and Birmingham, and goes to St Winifrid's Girls' School on the edge of Millford. I've seen

31

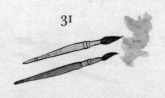

the St Winifrid's girls in town, immaculate in their bottle-green blazers and below-the-knee green kilts, their white ankle socks and shiny black lace-up brogues. Bobbi-Jo doesn't seem to fit the picture, but what do I know?

'My passion is music, obviously,' Bobbi-Jo tells us. 'I live for music – it's my way of expressing myself. I've played several instruments in the past. Playing keyboards is quite new for me, but I am a quick learner, and I'd love to be part of the Lost & Found. I think you have something special. I think you could go all the way to the top, and I want to be a part of that!'

Marley looks over at us, his mouth twitching into a grin.

'Why music?' he asks. 'What makes music so special?'

'I guess it's in my blood,' Bobbi-Jo explains with a shrug. 'My dad is Barney Bright, the star DJ on Millford Sounds Radio. You've probably heard of him. He used to manage a famous pop band, the Bright Boys.'

The rest of us exchange glances, and I can tell that it's not just me who's never heard of the Bright Boys.

'That was back in the nineties,' Bobbi-Jo admits. 'They haven't done much lately, but I know Dad's always looking for the next big thing. Mum used to be a stylist for photo shoots and music videos, so I've grown up with the music world all around me, really. They know I'm auditioning today, and they're rooting for me. They saw the news coverage of the festival and they think you're a band with shedloads of potential. My dad would just love to get you all on his radio show!'

Marley looks like he might explode with joy.

'Really? That's brilliant to hear!' he says. 'We've had quite a few applicants today, Bobbi-Jo, as you can imagine, but I think I speak for us all when I say that you seem like a perfect fit for the Lost & Found. We're rehearsing every day throughout the summer, from six until eight. I see you don't live in Millford itself – would that be a problem?'

'I'll just get the train in,' Bobbi-Jo says. 'I do that most days anyway. No hassle.'

'In that case,' Marley declares, 'welcome to the band!'

'Hang on,' Lexie cuts in. 'I mean – you seem like a great candidate, Bobbi-Jo, but before we make a final decision could we see you play? Did you prepare a piece?'

'Oh! Yes, sure! I am quite new to keyboards, but . . .'

'No worries, Bobbi-Jo,' Marley says. 'Just do what you can!'

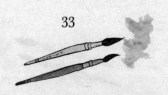

Sadly, what Bobbi-Jo can do is not good.

We're not expecting miracles, but she can barely play at all and it's hard to work out what the tune is supposed to be. Over and over, she bashes out the wrong notes, plays in the wrong key. She stops abruptly, starts in the wrong places, accidentally switches to booming church-organ mode and almost deafens us all. By the time she crashes to a standstill, we're all staring, speechless. Bobbi-Jo may have all the right connections, but she doesn't have a musical bone in her body.

'I don't actually have a keyboard at home,' she says, aware that we're not convinced. 'I've been learning on the school one, but – well, maybe I'm a bit rusty now that it's the holidays. I'm usually much better, promise!'

There's an awkward silence, and everyone looks at Marley. This is his chance to tell Bobbi-Jo he's made a mistake, been too hasty, that he'll have to think again. Marley loves the Lost & Found. There's no way he'd let the sound we've worked so hard to perfect be wrecked.

It turns out I am wrong about that.

'Great,' Marley says. 'Like you say, it just needs practice and perseverance. We can help you!'

Bex rolls her eyes and steps up alongside Marley. 'I'm not sure,' she says. 'We need to make sure we get the right person. We'll have a band meeting and let you know, Bobbi-Jo, OK?'

Bobbi-Jo frowns. 'OK,' she says. 'Do that! Just don't leave it too long, because another band want me too, and I won't be able to fob them off for long. They're an up-and-coming local rap band called Pretty Street – you've probably heard of them. They're tipped for great things. I'd much rather be with the Lost & Found, but if you're not sure . . .'

'We're sure,' Marley says. 'Absolutely certain. Bobbi-Jo, welcome to the Lost & Found!'

'Wow, wow, wow!' Bobbi-Jo squeals, flinging her arms around Marley and blowing air kisses to the rest of us. 'I can't believe it!'

'Neither can I,' Bex mutters darkly.

I don't think any of us can.

My father was a tailor in Damascus before the war. Every day he wore a blue pinstripe suit with an ancient label stitched inside that said Savile Row. 'It's where every smart English gentleman goes to buy his suits,' he'd declare. 'I learned from the best!'

My mother would look up from her sewing and roll her eyes and shake her head, but I was very proud of my father. 'When exactly did you live in London?' I had asked him once. 'Was it before you got married?'

My father just smiled and stroked his beard.

'Well, now I never actually lived in London,' he admitted. 'But your grandfather did — your mother was born there, and her older brother Dara lives there still. They had a tailor's shop on Savile Row . . . still do, I suppose. We lost touch with them a long time ago.'

'How come?' I asked.

'It was a row over money,' my mother said. 'After my father and mother and I came back to Syria, my brother Dara sent us money to open the shop in Damascus. It seems Dara said the money had been a loan and asked for it back, but my father was very angry and disowned him. I was still a child then — I don't suppose we'll ever know what really happened.'

She showed me an old photograph of a man and woman dressed in wedding finery, the only picture she had of Dara and his bride Zenna. 'It was a long time ago,' she said. 'We came back to Syria when I was seven.'

'If you hadn't, we'd never have met,' my father said, and he was lost in the past again, telling the story of how he'd been apprenticed at my grandfather's tailor's shop when he was seventeen years old, how he'd fallen in love with my mother and married her soon after. When my grandfather died, they'd inherited the business.

'I married the girl of my dreams,' my father declared. 'I'm the luckiest man alive!'

5

The Leaping Llama

An hour later, a gang of us are installed in a corner booth at the Leaping Llama, Marley's favourite hipster cafe – we all pitched in our spare cash and Lexie took it to the counter to order.

'I've got us all lemonades and a slice of chocolate fudge cake with seven spoons so we can share,' she says, sliding into the seat beside me. 'Like, maybe one bite each? Is that OK?'

'It is OK,' I say quietly, taking a sharp breath in. 'Thank you!'

Lexie looks back at me for a long moment, and the noise and chatter of the cafe falls away. I notice that her brown

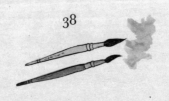

eyes have swirls of amber in them, that her lashes are longer than any I have ever seen, that her skin smells of sunshine and vanilla. I resist the impulse to edge sideways, closer to Jake, in case I smell of old coat or dry-cleaning fluid.

'They still arguing?' Lexie asks, and I nod and shrug, because this scrap shows no sign of easing up. Bex is in total meltdown, and I think it may take more than shared chocolate fudge cake to sort her out.

'I just don't get you, Marley Hayes!' she says. 'You are so, so out of order! You act like the Lost & Found is your own personal band, but it's not – we're all in it together. Choosing new members should be a joint decision, but you have to ignore that and pick Bobbi-Jo, who is possibly the most unmusical person we auditioned!'

'I didn't want to lose her to that other band, Pretty Street,' Marley argues.

'I have never heard of Pretty Street before,' Bex snaps. 'And neither have you, Marley – be honest!'

'Why did you even want us at the auditions if you weren't going to give us a say in the decision making?' Jake asks. 'And why choose someone who can't even hold a tune? I don't get it, Marley. You're supposed to care about this band!'

39

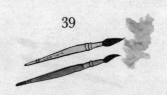

Marley looks uncomfortable. 'I'll sort it,' he mutters. 'I can get her up to scratch – stop stressing! Trust me, she'll be a big asset to the band!'

Dylan frowns. 'I think I get it,' he says. 'You and Lexie split up, didn't you? A few weeks back?'

'It's not a secret,' Lexie says, shrugging. 'Things just weren't working out.'

'Sadly, they weren't,' Marley says. 'Yes, we've split – so what?'

'So I think you're lining up Bobbi-Jo Bright to be your next girlfriend,' Dylan ploughs on. 'There has to be some attraction, and it sure as heck isn't her musical skills!'

'You're wrong, little brother,' Marley growls. 'You have no idea how wrong you are.'

'You do have a bit of a bad rep with girls,' Bex points out. 'And you've just turned down four applicants who could actually play in favour of one who can't. Don't get me wrong, Marley – I'm a feminist and I am all for a strong female presence in the band – but Bobbi-Jo can't play a single note!'

'She reckons she's a fast learner,' Marley says.

'I bet,' Bex mutters darkly.

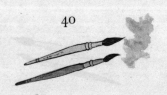

A waiter with a man bun arrives with a tray and starts setting out lemonade in jam-jar glasses with striped paper straws; the chocolate cake is served on a piece of slate with the promised seven spoons. The Leaping Llama is so hipster it's almost a joke – there's no way I'd come here normally. It's way out of my comfort zone and I'm not sure if it makes me want to laugh or cry. I think back to two years ago when I was eating food parcel rations of rice and beans cooked over roadside fires, and wonder again just how come I managed to reach safety when so many of those I travelled with did not. I guess it must be luck, or fate or a miracle.

I fish out my fineliner pen and settle for sketching a tiny portrait of the waiter, complete with topknot and tray held high, on the crumpled till receipt.

'Let's change the subject,' Lexie pleads. 'I hate it when we all fall out. I wanted to talk to you guys about Romy – it's her birthday on Saturday. Me, Happi and Bex thought we should do something to celebrate. We all know she has a tough time at home, what with looking after her mum and everything. What if we mark it somehow, make it special?'

Romy keeps quiet about her home life, but her mum is wheelchair-bound and it's clear the two of them struggle

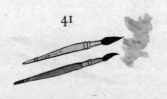

to cope. Like me, she didn't really have friends at school until she joined the Lost & Found – the band is a real lifeline for her.

'OK,' Marley says, looking relieved at the change of tack. 'I get it. What are we thinking?'

Lexie spoons up a piece of chocolate cake. 'A surprise party, maybe?' she suggests. 'At the old railway carriage – think fairy lights and bunting and blankets on the grass. It's the perfect venue, right? Romy turns up on Saturday expecting a rehearsal, and instead it's a party!'

'I'll make a birthday cake,' Happi offers. 'We can all chip in, bring a dish to share or a packet of crisps or something . . .'

'Cool,' Lexie says. 'Jake, can you tell Louisa Winter? Make sure she doesn't mind? We could call Romy's mum and see if she wants to come too. I'll ask Lee to do a playlist – and, Sami, I was going to ask if you could make a card with some of your little sketches on it. Something we can all sign?'

'Sketches?' I echo.

'Your drawings.' Lexie picks up the till receipt with the cartoon waiter inked on it. 'Like this one and the things you draw at band practice; cartoons of us all, scribbled on

42

music paper or in your notebook. You're really good, Sami! Everyone thinks so!'

There it is again, that shy smile that tugs at my deep-freeze heart.

'Sure,' I say, and I watch her eyes light up. 'No problem!'

Talk turns to who will bring what food and who has bunting or fairy lights at home, and I risk another glance at Lexie and catch her watching me. Her cheeks flush pink and she looks away, but suddenly my heart is racing. A wisp of something like hope unfurls inside me, but I push it away before it can take root. I have no business hoping that a crush could ever be more than that, not when my heart is covered with a thick layer of permafrost.

'So, Marley,' Bex says, steering back into dangerous waters. 'Will you be bringing your new girlfriend along? The one who can't play keyboards to save her life?'

'The one with two parents in the music business, more like,' Marley points out. 'They could be useful contacts. But no, we won't be dating – I promise you that.'

'Who are you trying to convince?' Bex says. 'You'll be dating before the week is out, I guarantee it. You've had more girlfriends than I've had hot dinners!'

'Leave it, Bex,' Marley says. 'You're way off. Seriously.'

'Tell them,' Lexie says quietly. 'You keep saying you're waiting for the right moment. Just do it, Marley.'

'Do what?' Bex echoes.

Lexie shrugs. 'Nothing,' she says, backtracking. 'It was just an idea.'

'What was?'

Marley rolls his eyes.

'Actually,' he says, 'Lexie's right. There's something I need to tell you all. And I need you to listen, and not judge.'

'Bit rich, coming from you,' Bex quips, but Lexie shakes her head, and Bex is silent.

'There's no easy way to say this,' Marley begins. 'You know I'm an idiot. You know I'm shallow, you know I'm ambitious, you know I can be a bit of a slave-driver . . .'

'Stop bigging yourself up,' Dylan jokes.

'I'm being serious,' Marley mutters. 'I'm not perfect, right? But there's something about me you don't know, and we're all mates, so, well, I want to tell you.'

Marley's usual confidence and charm have slipped, and he seems anxious, edgy. He's talking too fast, his fingers drumming against the tabletop.

44

'This is scary,' he is saying. 'You might think badly of me, or laugh at me, but I want you to know that I won't be going out with Bobbi-Jo, not in a week's time – not ever, OK? I won't be going out with any girls from now on because I'm tired of pretending to be something – someone – I'm not.'

'I don't get it,' Dylan says. 'Nobody said you were pretending!'

Marley looks anguished. 'But I was,' he says. 'I've been pretending ever since I can remember. And I'm sick of it!'

'Hang on,' Jake cuts in, frowning. 'You said something about not going out with girls. What are you trying to say, Marley?'

Across the table from me, Marley's cheeks flare crimson and his eyes look too bright, panicked.

'Look, there's no easy way to say this,' he pushes on. 'I'm still the same person, but the truth is . . . well, the truth is . . . I'm gay. I like boys, not girls, and I want to stop lying about it. OK?'

A stunned silence descends. I really didn't see Marley's revelation coming. Even before I knew him properly, Marley was famous in Millford Park Academy for three things: he

45

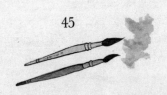

liked to fight; he was music mad; and he changed his girlfriends the way the rest of us change our socks.

I'd never have guessed Marley's secret in a million years, but I can feel how scared he is about our reaction, and I can see from Lexie's face that she knew already.

'Dude, are you kidding me?' Dylan whispers, but Marley just shakes his head.

'This doesn't change anything,' Jake says, nudging Marley in a play-fight kind of way.

'No, it doesn't,' Bex agrees. 'You're still an idiot!'

'But you're our idiot,' I quip. Marley snorts back a laugh, and I feel good for making my friend smile.

'Thanks for telling us,' Happi says. 'It can't have been an easy thing to share.'

We raise our jam-jar glasses and drink a toast to Marley, all except Lexie, who throws her arms round him and holds on tight. I am mean enough, just for a moment, to feel a sharp pang of envy.

'Perhaps one day we will visit London,' my father once said. It was evening, and we were up on the roof, cooling down beneath the stars. I was playing the flute, and the bright, clear notes fell around us like silk.

'We could visit Dara and Zenna, let the kids meet their cousins,' my father went on. 'We can see the sights – Buckingham Palace, the Tower of London, Edinburgh Castle!'

'Edinburgh Castle isn't in London,' my mother scoffed. 'Besides, I barely remember Dara. He's fifteen years older than me, and probably still angry about that loan . . .'

'We could put that right, patch things up,' my father said. 'Dara's argument was never with us, and your father is long gone. Dara is family!'

'But so far away!' my mother said.

My father just laughed and looked skyward. 'Not so very far,' he answered. 'Damascus or London, we all live under the same stars!'

My father reached up to the sky and pretended to pick out a star for my little sister Roza. She was five years old then, and she laughed and prised his fingers open, her eyes huge with wonder. In my father's palm shone a silver star, glinting in the moonlight.

I put down my flute and smiled.

The star was made of thin metal snipped from an old Coca-Cola tin, the sharp edges folded tightly back. It hadn't really come from the sky above us, but still, in a certain light, it seemed to shine with possibilities.

Later, my father showed me how to make a star from tin, how to score and fold and smooth the jagged edges. I cut my fingers and made them bleed, but eventually I turned the rubbish into silver.

'See?' my father said. 'Magic!'

6

Stars

It's Saturday evening and the party is in full swing. Fairy lights and home-made bunting are strung through the trees, and people crowd around a trestle table draped in a crumpled white sheet and laden with plates of sandwiches, crisps, salads, sausage rolls and my own contribution, a dish of hummus and some flatbreads made by Aunt Zenna.

The whole Lost & Found crew is here – Sasha is back from her caravan holiday in Wales and George is home from Portugal, both full of stories, both mildly astonished to meet Bobbi-Jo Bright, the worst keyboard player in the world. Romy's mum is here, her wheelchair draped with a pink feather boa, chatting away to Jake's mum, stepdad and little sisters. A hippy-dippy couple called Laurel and Jack are pouring her some elderflower cordial.

'She's coming!' Happi shrieks, and everyone falls silent as we turn to look at Romy approaching through the trees. She halts at the edge of the clearing, looking first baffled and then wide-eyed as she scans around and realizes this gathering is for her.

'Happy birthday, Romy!' we roar, and party poppers snap and explode all around us as Romy comes closer.

'What . . . what is this?' she asks, faltering.

'A birthday party for a very special girl,' her mum replies. Romy starts to laugh, just as Lee's playlist booms out into the summer evening and Happi comes down the steps of the old railway carriage carrying a chocolate cake with thirteen candles on it. Romy, it turns out, is the youngest in her school year and the youngest in the band.

Everybody sings 'Happy Birthday' and she leans across to blow out the candles and make a wish, and I find myself smiling, slightly bemused. It seems bizarre to me that I am here, at a birthday party for the only girl I know who is actually more of a loner than I am. England surprises me over and over, but my friends in the band are good people,

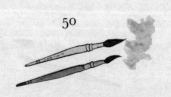

kind people. This party is something I am glad to be part of. Romy's eyes are shining as she finds herself the centre of attention for once.

A few months back, I made some Coke-can stars for my cousin Faizah's little boy. He was three years old, and probably too young for them, because when she thought I wasn't looking I saw Faizah snatch the stars away and drop them into the bin. Maybe she thought he'd eat them,

As everybody settles again, eating cake and drinking lemonade, I notice Romy drift to the edge of the gathering, back to her comfort zone. I make my way across to her, and she smiles, shyly.

'That card!' she exclaims as I approach. 'I can't . . . I don't think I've ever had a handmade card before, and this one is a work of art!'

She pulls it out of her shoulder bag and studies the collage of torn sheet music with little ink sketches of her playing violin drawn on top, gazing at the messages and signatures inside. 'I'm going to frame it and put it on my bedroom wall. I've never had a party before, not like this. You've all been so kind!'

'Lexie, Bex and Happi did most of the hard work,' I say,

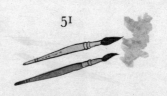

awkward now. 'It's a long time since I've been to a party, so this is strange for me too. I made you something else . . .'

I hand her a tissue-wrapped parcel of Coke-can stars, and watch her take out the little tin stars, looking at them with awe. Somehow, I don't think these will end up in the bin.

'For luck,' I tell her.

'Where's the birthday girl?' someone shouts, and Bobbi-Jo appears. She hooks an arm through Romy's and pulls her over to the makeshift dance floor beneath the trees. Romy looks terrified as the new girl drags her into an energetic cross between a jive and a conga, but Lexie, Bex, Happi and Sasha rush to her rescue and soon the six of them are whirling about to the sound of Pharrell's 'Happy'. Romy's look of horror has been replaced by laughter.

Why not? She has a pocketful of stars, after all.

I don't know much of Romy's story, but I know her life is not a breeze. Lexie and Bex are outsiders too, because of being in foster care, and Happi is far from your average Millford Park student with her ultra-strict and ultra-religious parents. Then there's George, with his horn-rimmed hipster glasses and bad skin, and Jake, who lived in a yurt until

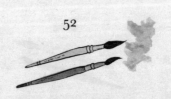

quite recently and used to come to school looking crumpled with his hair sticking up, and Lee who is always kind of hyper and clowns about all the time.

Once he blew his trumpet right in my ear when I wasn't expecting it, just for a joke, and I dropped to the floor, shaking, because it reminded me of the barrel-bomb attack that killed my friend Azif, back home in Syria. Lee was really sorry about it, obviously, and I guess he wasn't to know.

The point is, the Lost & Found is a collection of musical misfits, outsiders. Most of us really *are* lost, but we stick together and support each other. Even Marley has been keeping secrets, although everyone has made a point of assuring him that we don't really care whether he likes girls or boys, that we love him anyway, apart from his slave-driver tendencies and his obsessive drive for fame, fortune and musical world domination.

'Don't lie, you love all that stuff about me too,' Marley quips to Bex, and she flings a cushion at his head. That is actually quite restrained for her.

Bobbi-Jo is the only one who doesn't seem to have been told the news, and tonight she is flirting madly, batting her eyelashes as she flings herself around the makeshift dance floor. Marley seems totally clueless, but still, I can't help hoping that my crush on Lexie is a little less obvious.

What makes some people fall for each other and others not? I wish I knew.

I am surrounded by kids who could definitely be friends if only I would let them . . . and then there's Lexie, who could be more than a friend if I just had the courage to take a risk and let myself open up a little. I just don't think I can.

I glance back to the dancers, now joined by the hippy-dippy couple, Jake's little sisters and Marley himself, doing a slightly terrifying version of the cheesy old YMCA dance. Lexie has vanished.

I look around and spot her through the trees, sitting on a little wall beside the steps to the big house, some distance from the party. In the fading light she looks very small and very alone, and I find myself walking over. I have no idea what I might say or do, but that doesn't seem to matter.

'Sami,' she says, as I approach. 'Good party, huh? I think Romy's having fun!'

'She is,' I agree. 'You've made her very happy!'

'Not just me,' Lexie argues. '*All of us.* The whole Lost & Found gang. Teamwork, huh?'

'So why are you on your own?' I ask.

Lexie laughs. 'I'm on tortoise watch . . . I brought my pet tortoise, Mary Shelley. She likes to get out and about. Look – she's over there, just under the rose bush.'

I follow Lexie's gaze and spot a small grey-brown tortoise rustling about in the flower beds. It's unexpected, and it makes me smile.

'She likes strawberries,' Lexie says, opening her palm to offer me one. 'Among other things. See if she'll take it from you!'

I take a small strawberry and crouch down to offer it to the tortoise, grinning as she stretches up her scaly little head and blinks, as if deciding whether or not to trust me. In the end, the strawberry wins out, and she steps forward and snatches the little red fruit with a speed that makes me laugh.

'I didn't know you had a tortoise,' I say, sitting down on the wall beside Lexie. 'Especially not a famous Gothic novelist tortoise!'

'You've heard of Mary Shelley?' she asks. 'Hardly anyone

at school has! Have you read *Frankenstein*? I don't suppose
. . . did they have it in Syria?'

'I'm sure they did,' I say. 'But I read it in English. I
borrowed it from Bridge Street Library.'

'*I* got it from Bridge Street too!' Lexie exclaims. 'How
weird is that? When I was ten. Miss Walker the librarian
told me it might be too old for me, but I was pretty stubborn.'

I think for a moment of the weeks I spent reading that
book, sitting on the rickety old fire escape behind my uncle's
shop, huddled in my overcoat beneath a sky rendered
starless by orange street lights. I'd read slowly, with a
dictionary at my side, hooked by the story's darkness and
sorrow and the outcast monster who is all alone. It was a
book that chimed with me and gave me strength, and it
kind of freaks me out to know that Lexie had held exactly
the same library book in her hands a couple of years earlier.

'Miss Walker told me it might be too hard for me, also,'
is all I say. 'But I loved it. I am better at reading English
than speaking it.'

'You're great at speaking it,' she counters. 'You're just . . .
well, quiet. I don't blame you. Hard to get a word in
edgeways with that lot!'

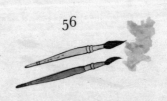

'They are good people,' I say.

'They are,' she agrees. 'Mad as a box of frogs, sometimes, but basically cool.'

'And yet . . . you sit here, away from your friends, alone?' I say. 'Are you very sad about Marley?'

Lexie laughs. 'About Marley being gay?' she checks. 'No, I'm really, really not. I've known for a few weeks now, and it actually makes a lot of sense. I'm glad he's told everybody. He can start to be himself, stop trying to be something he isn't. It's a good thing.'

'But still . . . still you are sad?' I push.

Lexie jumps up and runs a few steps into the greenery, scooping up Mary Shelley and holding her close. 'I'm often sad, Sami,' she says softly in the twilight. 'I try not to be, and it's not all the time, but . . . I miss my mum. Sometimes, things like this catch me unawares, remind me of the past. It must be a bit like that for you.'

The words catch in my throat. 'A bit like that,' I reply.

Abruptly, the front door of Greystones House opens, casting a pool of light, and Louisa Winter, the eccentric artist who owns the place, appears at the top of the steps. She's a striking woman, dramatic in a blue linen tunic

57

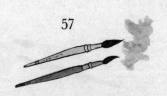

layered over an embroidered skirt, her long auburn hair swept up into a messy knot secured with paintbrushes. She is holding a bowl of chocolate-drenched pastries and a small ribbon-wrapped gift.

'Children!' she exclaims, as if we're both five years old. 'How nice to see you! And your famous tortoise, of course, Lexie. How lovely to meet her at last! I'm just going down to the party. I have some profiteroles for everybody, and a little present for Romy. It's a silk scarf – a vintage Biba one. D'you think she'll like it?'

'She'll love it,' Lexie says.

Louisa walks down the steps and heads through the trees towards the fairy lights and the music and the buzz of laughter.

'What exactly is a vintage Biba scarf?' I ask Lexie.

'No idea!'

She pads across the grass and sits down beside me on the wall, holding the tortoise on her knee. She is so close I find myself inhaling her sunshine and vanilla smell again, and just for a moment it makes me feel dizzy.

'Where did you get her?' I ask, keeping my voice steady.

'Mary Shelley.'

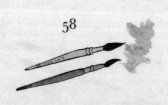

'She wandered into my foster family's garden on my eleventh birthday,' she tells me. 'Nobody ever claimed her – I think it was fate. I looked her up on the internet . . . she's a Hermann's tortoise. They live in the Mediterranean, mostly. She's a long way from home.'

I know that feeling.

'She was lost and I rescued her,' Lexie is saying. 'I like to rescue lost stuff. Books, things, pets, people . . .'

The words come tumbling out before I can stop them: 'I wish someone would rescue me.'

Lexie's eyes snag on mine, then slide away again, shining in the half-light. A dark curtain of hair falls across her face, and she dips down to place Mary Shelley on the grass at the foot of the steps.

'I guess I could try,' she whispers softly, then leans across and kisses me.

'Why do you always use the same lining fabric for your suits?' I asked my father, once. 'Why always grey? Why not blue, or cream or green?'

'Not grey, Sami,' he corrected me. 'My trademark is silver linings – a little bit of luxury and magic in an uncertain world!'

He stopped pinning the jacket he was working on, took a bolt of silver-grey fabric from the shelf and shook it out across the workbench, a sea of glinting satin.

My little sister Roza caught the end of the fabric and wrapped it around her like a silver shawl, dancing around the workshop. It made my father laugh.

'Life is unpredictable,' he said. 'Things don't always work out the way you think, but no matter what happens, you can always find a silver lining. Once upon a time I dreamed of going to London, but instead I married a girl who was born there . . . my Yasmine was the most beautiful girl in the world. She still is.'

Roza giggled and my mother rolled her eyes, but I could see her trying to hide a smile.

'I am a lucky man, Sami, and a happy one,' my father said. 'Who is to say we won't make it to London one day and open our own little business?'

'Dreamer,' my mother said, shaking her head.

'Perhaps I am,' my father replied. 'What do we have but dreams when it comes to it? Our hopes and dreams will still be here, long after we are gone.'

Roza stopped dancing and stepped back, and my father smoothed the grey satin fabric across the workbench, took the sharp scissors and sliced into it.

'Look for the silver linings, Sami,' he told me. 'They are always there if you look hard enough. And never be afraid to take a risk for love. It might not come around a second time!'

I always looked for silver linings after that, and the truth in things, but I had never taken a risk for love.

7

Take a Risk

The kiss is perfect. The touch of warm lips on mine, soft fingers trailing across my skin, the smell of vanilla and the taste of birthday cake still on her lips . . . but I am frozen. I'm a human glacier, made of ice and moving at a rate of one centimetre every hundred years. Two, three seconds go by, or possibly two or three lifetimes, and I'm motionless, stuck, just letting it happen.

By the time I recover the ability to react, it's over, and shame floods through me like poison. This is what happens when your heart is in the deep freeze.

Lexie jumps up and runs across the grass, chasing a

runaway tortoise. I watch her scoop up Mary Shelley and turn to face me in the dusk.

'Sami,' she says. 'I shouldn't have . . . I don't even . . . I'm an idiot, OK? Forget that happened!'

I want to tell her she *should* have, that she's *not* an idiot – I am, and that I won't be able to forget, but she's gone, running through the dusk towards the music and the glinting lights of the party.

Over the next few days, I tell myself to forget it, like Lexie said. She kissed me, I froze, it was awkward and she ran away. I'd have to be mad to wade back in there when my feelings have been stuck in the permafrost for so long, when I don't even know if a thaw is possible. I've watched the kids at Millford Park. Some of them have a different partner every week . . . it makes romance look like a fast track to getting hurt all over again.

Still . . . it was my first kiss. That's not the kind you forget in a hurry. And Lexie . . . well, she's not like anyone else I know.

Take a risk, the shadow of my father's voice says. *Take a risk.*

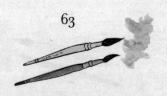

Could I?

My head fills up with plans to make things right, to try to explain, to start over and ask Lexie on a date. The problem is that I hardly ever see her alone: at band practice we're just two kids of a dozen; the rest of the time, she's with Happi and Bex, or talking music and lyrics with Marley. I try to pluck up the courage to call for her, but before I'm halfway along the street I spot Bex sitting on the doorstep reading a brick-like copy of *War and Peace*, and my courage melts away. I march on past, throwing Bex a gruff nod, as if I'm on my way to an urgent appointment and had no idea they happened to live en route.

Take a risk, my father had said, but I guess he'd never met Bex with her dip-dyed hair and her Doc Marten boots and her acid tongue. I could stand in their garden at midnight and throw pebbles at the bedroom window, but knowing my luck Bex would appear and chuck a bucketful of water over me.

In the end I do what every other kid at Millford Park Academy does and send a text message. It takes every scrap of bravery I have.

Sami:	I am not very good at being rescued, am I? Could we try again?

Minutes tick by. An hour. I am helping my uncle in the workshop, taking up the hem on a pair of tweed trousers, repairing a tear on the sleeve of a designer jacket, letting out the seams on a bridesmaid's dress made from pale orange polyester. It's not difficult work for me; I am used to it. I've always loved the care and precision needed, taken pride in making something look good as new. My father said I had a talent for it. My uncle says my work is better than anything he or Aunt Zenna can do, and I tell him that my mother was better still, that she could take a roll of fabric and turn it into something magical.

'I wish I'd known her as an adult,' Uncle Dara says. 'My father wanted to go home to Syria, and of course he took Yasmine too – she was only a child, the baby of the family. And then there was the falling out . . .'

'What happened?' I dare to ask. 'My mother said it was about money,'

Uncle Dara sighs. 'My father needed money for the flight

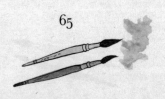

home,' he explained. 'And money to open his shop in Damascus. This place was just rented back then, so I took out a series of loans to help him. He didn't pay me back, and when I asked for the money he got angry and disowned me. It was a great sadness for me that he could do that, but perhaps by then he was already ill?'

'Perhaps,' I say. I knew that my grandfather had suffered from dementia in his last years. It seems so sad that it could have caused him to push away his only son.

'I grew up believing that you had a tailor's shop on Savile Row in London, not a dry-cleaner's shop in Millford,' I tell him. 'It's a miracle I managed to find you!'

'I'm glad you did, Sami,' Uncle Dara says.

I'm glad too, of course, but there's such a tangle of conflicting emotions inside me that all I manage is a sad smile.

My mobile buzzes at last.

Lexie: Try again? What would that involve?

I sigh. Is that a knockback? A challenge?

66

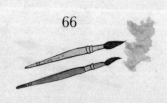

Sami:	I would say sorry. Explain why I'm such an idiot. We could go on a date. Maybe?
Lexie:	Maybe . . .

I smile. I can hear my father's voice, telling me to take a risk.

Sami:	I am sorry things were awkward. You don't have to rescue me. I am probably a lost cause anyway. I am a mess, but I like you very much. Would you like to go out some time? Maybe? Take a risk?

Ten whole minutes go by. The waiting is torture. When my mobile finally buzzes I stab myself with a needle and almost bleed all over a freshly washed and ironed white shirt.

Lexie:	Today then, after band practice?

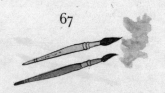

I laugh out loud, then punch an arm in the air and whoop.

I tell my aunt and uncle I am going out, and lock myself in the bathroom to get ready. I take the longest shower ever, then borrow some of Aunt Zenna's conditioner in an attempt to tame my hair. I iron a clean T-shirt, put on my best pair of supermarket skinny jeans.

I look in the mirror and see the reflection of a tall, thin boy with a tangle of wavy dark hair, a long nose with nostrils that flare, grey eyes that burn, lips that have tasted tears too many times. This is clearly not movie-star material, but I suppose it could be worse. Then I look down, and there's the overcoat, frayed at the cuffs and worn at the seams, with blotchy stains from the Aegean Sea and Greek sand and Macedonian mud in spite of the time I spent earlier brushing and swabbing it with my uncle's dry-cleaning fluid.

The coat has definitely seen better days.

'For goodness' sake, Sami, just leave it behind for once!' Aunt Zenna says as I pass through the living room. 'You look lovely, but that coat – no, no, no! It's August; there's a heatwave out there. Nobody needs a coat in this weather!'

'It's not about the weather,' I say.

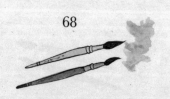

'I know it's not,' Uncle Dara says. 'We know that the coat means a great deal to you, Sami, of course we do. But you must see that soon this coat will fall apart, no matter how carefully you try to mend it. No matter how special it is to you, Sami, you will lose it if you wear it every day. Perhaps we should wrap it in tissue paper and hang it in the wardrobe, keep it safe?'

'One day,' I tell him. 'Perhaps.'

'OK,' my uncle agrees. 'I'm just asking that you think about it, Sami, that's all.'

'I will think about it.'

I turn back to the mirror, rake a hand through my hair.

'Your hair needs cutting too,' Aunt Zenna chips in. 'You look like one of those pop stars from the seventies. If you'd just let me –'

I run out of the flat before she can grab a pair of scissors.

'Has Sami got a girlfriend?' I hear my uncle asking as I head down the stairs, and I can't help wondering the same thing.

If I've taken some time over my appearance, it's clear that Lexie has too. She always looks good, but today she's wearing a little black T-shirt with a red polka-dot skirt and

69

leggings, and has a gauzy red bow tied in her hair. She smiles and looks away, her cheeks pink.

'You look . . . different,' Bobbi-Jo tells her. 'Very original. Like Minnie Mouse!'

Lexie looks uncertain about whether this is a good thing or a bad thing, but she's the kind of girl who always sees the best in people and she gives Bobbi-Jo the benefit of the doubt. I'm not sure Bobbi-Jo deserves it – her face takes on a sneery look when she glances at Lexie. It looks for a moment as though she's going to take a dislike to Sasha too, but when our lead singer misses her cue for the first song, Marley shouts at her to wake up and pay attention, that she's not on holiday now, and Bobbi-Jo visibly relaxes. It's like she is trying to suss whether Sasha is any kind of threat to her, and she decides she's not.

I'm guessing that Bobbi-Jo still hasn't heard the newsflash that Marley is gay, because she has him targeted like a rabbit in the headlights. She is not about to give up. 'This song's quite tricky,' she says, looking at him from beneath her lashes. 'Can you show me again?'

'Just follow the tune,' Marley says, confused. 'Take it slow . . . and stop worrying. You'll pick it up!'

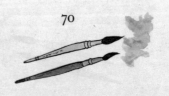

'We've all been there,' Lexie says helpfully. 'You should have heard some of our earlier practices . . . They were chaos!'

'What are you trying to say?' Bobbi-Jo snaps. 'That I'm making the band sound bad? That I'm chaotic?'

'Er . . . no, not at all!' Lexie says. 'I just thought you seemed worried about the song. I was only trying to say, give it time!'

Bobbi-Jo gives one of her slightly scary smiles. 'I'll be fine,' she says icily.

Bobbi-Jo is not fine, though. She crashes through the notes so clumsily that at times it sounds like an elephant has sat down on the keyboard, and she seems not to notice that she's out of time and out of tune. Maybe she is new to the keyboards, but that's not the problem; it's more that she has zero musical talent.

The old railway carriage is stifling in the summer heat, even with the door wide open. I've had enough of fighting the chaos for today. I set my flute down and take the notebook from my pocket, lean back and start to draw. I draw Romy first, her face lost in the music as she plays her violin, then Bex, tall and fierce with her bass guitar and her sea-green hair, anger brewing behind her eyes like a

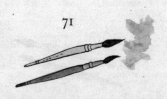

smouldering volcano. I draw Marley looking annoyed, and Bobbi-Jo, totally oblivious, her face radiant, crashing out an endless stream of bum notes. And I draw Lexie, of course, her pixie face serious beneath that shrunk-in-the-wash fringe as she sings backing vocals for the songs she and Marley have written together.

I notice that Lee has put down his trumpet, that Dylan is just going through the motions, drumming out a gloomy beat and smashing the hi-hat cymbal savagely every time Bobbi-Jo gets it wrong. Which is every few seconds.

'Enough,' Marley decrees at last. 'Stop, all of you. I think that's probably enough for today – it's just not working, is it? It's a shambles!'

The entire practice has lasted twenty minutes instead of the usual two hours, but it feels like an eternity.

'You probably need to get hold of a keyboard to practise at home,' Marley tells her. 'You have to get up to speed on the basics before you can slot in with the songs. It's not quite working yet.'

Bobbi-Jo looks stricken. 'I'll try harder,' she promises. 'And I'm sure Dad will buy me something to practise on. I'm sorry! I don't want to let you all down!'

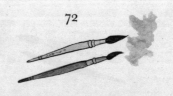

'You're not letting us down,' Marley says. 'But you do need to bring your playing up to scratch. How about we put in some extra practice here? I can help you go through the keyboard part for each song. Maybe simplify things a bit?'

'That would be wonderful!' she gushes. 'I'll do whatever it takes! Shall we do that now, Marley? Go through the songs one by one, just you and me?'

'Er, not right now,' Marley huffs. 'I've got a few things I need to sort. Can you fit in an extra practice tomorrow at five?'

'Of course!' Bobbi-Jo says, her smile about a mile wide. 'See you then, Marley. See you guys! Oh, Lexie, that bow – not being horrible, but it's just not working. It makes you look about seven years old!'

She stalks down the steps and off across the grass, leaving the rest of us feeling what Marley describes as 'gobsmacked'.

'You look lovely,' I tell Lexie, and, although she blushes a furious scarlet, her lips twitch into a smile. Everyone else turns to look at me, the quiet kid who has finally said something interesting. I shrug and raise an eyebrow and pick up my flute again.

'Sami's right,' Marley says. 'Take no notice, Lexie.

73

Bobbi-Jo is a bit . . . well, let's just say she's not quite what I expected.'

'No kidding,' Bex comments. 'She's a nightmare! Marley, you've messed up big time – you have to get rid of her before she ruins the band. We've worked so hard, and suddenly, thanks to her, we're back to square one. If Ked Wilder had heard that practice, he wouldn't touch us with a barge pole!'

'He'd have to have good hearing to hear it all the way from France,' Marley says. 'Some mentor he's turned out to be . . . Ms Winter says he'll be away all summer and doesn't want to be disturbed. Like it or not, we're on our own and we're just going to have to work extra hard to get ourselves noticed.'

'I think we'd better hope people don't notice us right now,' Lee comments. 'We'll need to hand out free earplugs pretty soon, if Bobbi-Jo stays in the band.'

'She just needs time to settle,' Marley says. 'I'll make sure she gets the hang of things. Her dad's a brilliant contact, and we need all the help we can get right now. Can't you see what a great opportunity this could be?'

Nobody seems convinced.

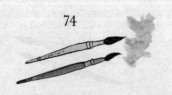

Marley sighs. 'We just have to be patient, give Bobbi-Jo a bit more time – I guarantee things will work out.'

'I guarantee they won't,' Bex says. 'Look, this is going nowhere. We've finished our practice early and the night is still young – shall we go and do something? Catch a movie or take a boat out on the lake? Cheer ourselves up?'

'Yes, let's,' Happi agrees. 'It's ages since we've done something like that!'

Jake suggests going bowling, and that meets with everyone's approval.

'Should we go?' Lexie asks me in a whisper. 'I've never been bowling before . . .'

'Me neither,' I tell her. 'We could go, if you want. Or we could just stay here?'

'Stay here,' she says under her breath. 'Yeah?'

'What's up?' Bex wants to know, catching the tail end of the conversation.

Lexie grins. 'I was just saying I don't think Bobbi-Jo likes me much. I mean, *Minnie Mouse*!'

'You don't look like Minnie Mouse,' Bex says. 'She's jealous. She must know you used to go out with Marley, and she's letting you know she's set her sights on him, that's all.'

75

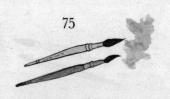

'Don't say that,' Marley groans. 'Can't she see I'm not interested?'

'Clearly not,' Lexie says. 'You're a born flirt, Marley. Looks like Bobbi-Jo is getting mixed messages. Just tell her!'

'I will,' he says. 'Probably . . .'

'Are you scared?' Happi asks. 'Do you think she'll judge you or something?'

'No, no, it's just . . . I don't know. I'm still getting used to it myself, that's all,' he explains. 'It was easier with you guys – you're proper friends. I don't know Bobbi-Jo so well. I *will* tell her, some time. Promise.'

'You're handling it all pretty well,' Jake comments. 'Respect, mate.'

Marley shrugs. 'I just feel better knowing it's not a secret any more,' he says. 'It was wearing me out, covering it up all the time, living a lie. Anyhow, bowling alley, right? Let's forget band stuff – and personal stuff – for a while!'

'Coming, Lexie?' Bex asks, and Lexie shrugs and says she's not in the mood, that she'll stay and tidy up and lock the old railway carriage behind her. She takes off the Minnie Mouse bow and stuffs it into her bag.

'Not a good look, clearly,' she says.

'I liked it,' I say.

Bex frowns, her eyes narrowing as if she can see a whole world of meaning behind that comment, but I keep my face blank and calm and she heads off with the others.

'Coming, Sami?' Marley asks, and I shrug and shake my head.

'I'll buy you a lemonade,' he offers. 'Bowling's a laugh – you'll like it!'

I follow him down the steps, scratching around for some kind of excuse to get me off the hook, but what's the point of lies and half-truths, of hiding things?

'I guess I'll wait for Lexie,' I say, sinking down on the steps. Marley gives me a long, hard look.

'Yeah,' he says at last. 'I reckon I could see that coming . . . you and Lexie. Just don't you dare hurt her, OK?'

'I won't,' I say, although I know it's a promise I may not be able to keep. When your heart is in the deep freeze, you've got no business going around pretending it's OK. Someone, somewhere is going to get hurt . . . I just really, really hope it won't be Lexie.

THINGS TO DO

★ A meal (chip shop?)

★ Feed the ducks in the park

★ Posh drink in a jam jar at the Leaping Llama

★ Cinema trip

★ Bicycle ride

★ Art gallery visit

★ Picnic in the park

★ Take Mary Shelley to the seaside

★ Stargazing

★ Eat ice cream from an ice-cream van — flakes and strawberry sauce optional

8

The List

The first thing you need to know about the list is that it's a lie. I don't want to do all those things, but it's hard to find something romantic to do on a date in Millford so I stuck in a few extra ideas to make it look better.

I do not want to go to the Leaping Llama, for example. It's a phoney kind of a place, where everything costs too much and everyone looks a certain way, and they're all busy trying to capture their visit on Twitter, Snapchat and Instagram. That doesn't make sense to me. The other thing I have no plans to do is go to the seaside, for obvious reasons. I can still remember the Greek sand crusting my wet skin as I crawled out of the sea three years ago. I can remember the soft touch of sunrise on my back, the taste of salt on my lips that could have been either seawater or tears. A seaside visit does not appeal.

I hear footsteps behind me, and Lexie appears in the doorway.

'So, what are we doing?' she asks, and I hand her the list to look at. She sits down beside me, grinning.

'All of this tonight?' she teases. 'Or are you saying we'll have ten dates?'

'I am an optimist,' I say, even though I'm not sure if I am, not any more. 'This is just for starters!'

'Let's get one date done,' Lexie says. 'We can see how we go from there.'

'I guess.'

There's a silence, and I feel a little sad, as though this whole idea is ridiculous, impossible.

'I love the little sketches,' Lexie says, looking at the list. 'They're amazing. I watch you, sometimes; you're always drawing at band practice, during the in-between bits. I'd love to see your sketchbook.'

But the little notebook in my coat pocket is filled with sadness. I am not ready to share that yet.

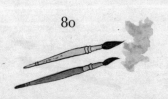

'Some day, perhaps,' I tell her. 'Back home in Damascus, my dream was to study art, perhaps become an illustrator. I don't think that will happen now.'

'I don't see why not,' Lexie says with a frown. 'You're easily good enough. I bet you'd get on to a degree course no bother, once you're older.'

I shrug. It's too difficult to explain just what I lost on the journey from Damascus to Millford – way more than just my family, my friends, my home. I lost my past and my future, my confidence, my courage, my dreams.

That's not a great topic for a first date, obviously.

'So what shall we do?' I ask, changing the subject. 'Chip shop? Feed the ducks? Watch a film? You choose!'

Lexie bites her lip.

'I'd just like to get to know you,' she says shyly. 'You're so quiet – you don't give much away. Sometimes I think there's something between us, and other times I'm not sure. But I think there could be. We have things in common – from what I've been told, we've both lost the people we love, and found new families we still struggle to fit in with . . .'

I nod. 'My uncle and aunt are very kind. I'm lucky to be

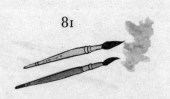

here with family who look after me, but sometimes I can't help thinking about what I've lost. Is that what it's like for you with your foster family?'

'A bit,' Lexie says. 'I kept them at arm's length for so long – it's hard to let people get close when you've been hurt.'

I take a deep breath. I want to ask if Lexie's heart is frozen too, but I'm scared to know the answer.

'Not long ago, I found out I had grandparents I never even knew about,' Lexie is saying. 'That was weird. It was actually Ms Winter who helped my grandparents to find me again – they'd been friends with her for years, but they didn't even know I existed until they saw that picture of me and the rest of the band in the *Millford Gazette* with Ms Winter and Ked Wilder. They recognized me – I look exactly like my mum used to, apparently.'

'That's so cool,' I say, meaning it but knowing that newly found grandparents probably can't replace Lexie's long lost mum. 'So what happens now? I mean, you're not going to live with them? Or are you?'

'I don't know,' Lexie admits. 'Maybe, eventually. Maybe not. I'd miss my foster parents, and Bex, obviously. I know

that my grandparents are family, but I didn't know a thing about them until a few weeks ago and it's early days . . .'

'I understand,' I say. 'That's kind of how I feel about Uncle Dara and Aunt Zenna. I'm grateful to be here. I'm so lucky compared to a lot of refugee kids, but I miss my parents and my sister so much – it's like part of me has been lost along with them. I want to feel lucky, I want to fit in, but how can I? I just don't belong.'

'Oh, Sami, you do,' she tells me. 'You're amazing. You're the bravest and most inspiring person I know – you've come through so much! Besides, the Lost & Found are all misfits, really, aren't we? I think that's why we make such a good team!'

Being a part of the Lost & Found is one of the best things about being in Millford, but I feel awkward and uncomfortable about the compliments. I don't want to be called brave or inspiring; it's too much, too soon. I want to rewind and find safer territory. Luckily, Lexie seems to understand.

'I'm going to shut up,' she says, grinning up at me from beneath that cute little fringe. 'I talk too much when I'm nervous. Let's take it slowly, OK?'

83

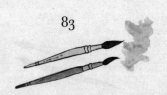

'OK. We can take this slowly too,' I say, nodding towards the list.

'I can't believe you made this for me,' she says. 'Even if we never do half of these ideas . . . well, it's still lovely.'

Her brown eyes are shining, her grin is wide and hopeful. She makes me believe we could have a chance, maybe, if we wanted to. She makes me want to take a risk.

'There is one thing I forgot to put on the list,' I say. 'Something I'd really like to do more than any of that other stuff . . .'

'What's that?' Lexie asks.

'It's just . . . this.'

My hand strokes her hair, soft as silk, and the evening sun picks out highlights of mahogany and golden brown I have never noticed before. I take a deep breath and lean my forehead against hers, and her hair falls forward, a soft, sleek curtain that touches my own bird's-nest tangle.

I breathe in sunshine and vanilla and some kind of citrus shampoo, and then our lips meet, and this time I don't freeze or panic.

My lips touch hers, softly. There's a slab of ice where my heart should be, and it aches so much I think it might

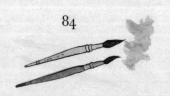

kill me, but then Lexie rests the palm of her hand right over the centre of my chest and all at once the ice is melting. Just like on those documentaries, the Arctic summer has finally arrived, and I'm so shocked at the overload of emotion I don't know what to do. My body is all floodwater, all feeling. I could drown in it. I remember reading a book about a man who had frostbite, about the pain he felt in his hands and feet as the sensation slowly returned, and I think that perhaps I feel like that. Still, the pain is worth it.

We pull apart, take a breath, but neither of us wants to be anywhere else but here. We look at each other, grinning like little kids, eyes wide, as if we are discovering something unique, something amazing . . . each other. My fingers trail down the soft skin of her cheek, brush the faint dusting of freckles across her nose. Her fingers slide across my cheekbones, trace the line of my jaw, burrow up into my hair. She laughs, and then we're kissing again, the list forgotten, everything forgotten except for this.

Arctic summers can be over in a heartbeat, of course, but I try not to think of that.

*

85

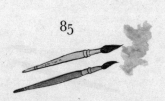

The next day, I am brushing my teeth in the bathroom, fresh from the shower, skin scrubbed and shiny-new. I drag on jeans and T-shirt, catch sight of my reflection in the mirror, my face half hidden behind a mess of damp hair. I swear I look different.

I'm the Arctic tundra, come to life at last, my heart a big mess of joy and pain, hammering in my chest, telling me I'm alive and I shouldn't waste a single minute. I pull in great lungfuls of air, laughing, and when Aunt Zenna raps on the bathroom door to ask if I'm OK, I open it and throw my arms around her, thank her for taking me in, for caring.

'What's wrong, Sami?' she asks. 'What's wrong?'

But nothing is wrong – just the opposite. For the first time since I arrived, everything is right. I tidy my room, make the bed and put my dirty clothes in the washing basket, then help Aunt Zenna with the breakfast dishes before heading out, a backpack stuffed with picnic food dangling from one shoulder.

Lexie and I have decided to work our way through the list after all, starting with a picnic in the park. I provide pita bread, my favourite yoghurt-cheese, lebna with za'atar, and

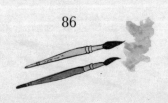

a dish of Aunt Zenna's best ful, made of fava beans. Lexie brings orange juice and apples and home-made flapjacks, plus a striped blanket to set them out on, and we meet under the willow tree beside the park lake.

There's the tiniest moment as we first catch sight of each other when it seems like we might be shy, but then we're grinning and Lexie runs at me like I'm some long-lost friend she hasn't seen in years, and I lift her up and whirl her around and I wonder how I ever got through the days without this girl in my life.

'You're so different!' she says. 'What happened, Sami?'

'You happened,' I tell her.

She blinks. 'Am I different too?'

'You're sort of . . . brighter,' I say, and she is. Her eyes are sparkling, her skin glows, her hair glints in the midday sun. I wonder if she's experiencing her own Arctic summer.

'We'll never be the same again,' she says, and I hope she's right.

My father taught me to sew early on. I'd sit in his lap, his arms around me, guiding my fingers as we stabbed the needle in and out of a piece of scrap fabric, stitching pathways of red woollen yarn across crumpled cotton. He was an exacting teacher.

'Stitches can be a kind of language,' he used to tell me. 'Strong, practical, creative, a way of connecting and constructing. A thread that pulls us all together, silent and invisible. This is an important skill, Sami. Concentrate!'

After a few years, I was neat enough and fast enough to stitch the finest seams. The whole family worked together to make the business succeed: my father, my mother, my little sister Roza and me. Often I would use the old Singer sewing machine to stitch the slippery grey satin fabric, making the trademark silver linings for my father's jackets.

By the time war came, there had been rumblings of discontent for a while. We didn't think it would affect us. We didn't think it would last. A change of government, a change of leader, and everything would go on as normal.

That didn't happen. People spoke of civil war, of revolution. Life as we knew it fell apart — everything changed.

People stopped ordering suits and coats and tunics because there were more pressing things to think of. Money dwindled, meals seemed to shrink, dust gathered on the windows of my father's shop. Everybody talked of politics and war, and I watched as my father's friends and clients turned against each other, taking different sides, choosing different opinions.

Slowly, we slipped into a nightmare world.

9

A Day in the Life

'Yassss,' Bex Murray announces as Lexie and I arrive for band practice. 'The lovebirds are here! Aww . . . cute, huh?'

A chorus of wolf whistles and giggles greets us as we make our way through the old railway carriage. I cringe at the attention but manage a smile, holding Lexie's hand more tightly.

'Bex,' she tells her foster sister through gritted teeth. 'Remind me never to tell you anything in confidence again! What are we, the gossip of the day?'

'My lips were sealed,' Bex says with a shrug. 'And then Happi mentioned that you'd texted her the news,

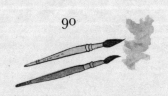

and Marley asked if anyone knew what was going on with the two of you, and . . . well, it just sort of came out! Oops!'

'Congratulations,' Happi says. 'I think you make a great couple!'

'Look after her, Sami, mate,' Marley grins. 'She's quite something!'

'I know that,' I say. 'I will.'

The Lost & Found settle down again, tuning instruments, getting ready to rehearse. I almost miss the venomous look Bobbi-Jo shoots at Lexie, and I realize that not everyone is pleased for us.

'Good luck,' she warns me quietly. 'I suppose Lexie's working her way through all the boys in the band . . . Some girls are like that.'

'Miaow,' Lee says, but thankfully nobody else seems to have heard. I am no expert on girls, but her spiteful comment seems more driven by annoyance at Marley's words than anything else.

I think that Bobbi-Jo Bright is a very insecure girl, and she really, really doesn't like Lexie.

*

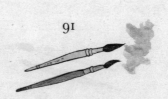

Yet another disastrous practice is limping to an early close when Louisa Winter raps sharply on the door of the railway carriage a few days later. She peeps inside, a vision in a paint-stained apron, her tumbledown hair today adorned with an impressive clutch of iridescent peacock feathers as well as the usual paintbrushes. She is grinning, eyes bright.

'Children – I've just picked up an answerphone message from Ked Wilder,' she announces. 'He called earlier on from his villa in France, but I was painting in my studio and must have missed his call . . .'

'He's still in France?' Marley checks. 'How much longer? Not being rude, but I was hoping he'd be around to give us some advice, maybe help us cut our first single . . .'

Ms Winter frowns. 'Ked spends every summer in Provence,' she says with just the faintest shadow of reproach. 'He always has, ever since he retired. This year, though, he's writing new material for the first time in more than two decades. He's asked not to be disturbed; we have to respect that.'

'Yeah . . . of course,' Marley says. 'Sorry – I'm impatient. Always have been.'

Ms Winter smiles. 'That's understandable, I suppose,'

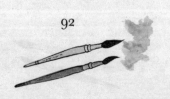

she says. 'I'm sure once Ked's back in the UK he'll be happy to advise you, but it won't be for a while. Anyway, he called to let me know that apparently that documentary's on tonight – the one they made at the festival!'

'A documentary?' Bobbi-Jo shrieks. 'About us? How cool!'

'About Ked Wilder,' Bex corrects her. 'And it was filmed weeks ago, at the festival . . . so not about "us", exactly.'

Not about *you*, Bex clearly means, but Bobbi-Jo seems not to notice.

Marley brightens. 'Tonight? Wow, I had no idea! What time?'

Ms Winter raises an eyebrow. 'That's the problem,' she explains, checking her watch. 'It's on any minute now. I thought I'd better tell you; it's on one of those odd music channels, so I don't think there've been any trailers for it.'

'Better abandon the practice and get home to watch,' Lee chips in. 'Although if it's starting now I'm going to miss the first fifteen minutes . . .'

'Come up to the house,' Louisa Winters decrees. 'Quickly, before we miss the whole thing. Come on!'

Five minutes later, we're all in the big, bohemian living room at Greystones, seated on Indian floor cushions,

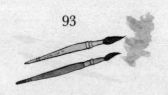

squashed on an L-shaped sofa in emerald velvet or sprawled across the threadbare Persian carpet, watching the flatscreen TV. Ms Winter has put a tray of mismatched glasses, a packet of chocolate digestives and a big jug of home-made lemonade on the coffee table, which isn't a table at all but a big, battered tin trunk decorated with antique stickers and luggage labels from places like Paris, Berlin, Kathmandu, Constantinople and Machu Picchu.

'My mother was a bit of an adventurer,' is all she says by way of a comment, and we help ourselves to lemonade and biscuits as the programme begins. *A Day in the Life of Ked Wilder*, it's called, and the narrator begins by outlining Ked's rise to fame in the 1960s, illustrated by a collage of images of the singer looking young and cool in skin-tight jeans and Chelsea boots, including one shot of him with a beautiful doe-eyed girl with hair in waist-length auburn waves hanging on his arm.

'It's *you*!' Lexie shrieks, looking at Ms Winter. 'Oh wow! This is brilliant!'

'Feels like yesterday,' Ms Winter muses. 'Where does the time go?'

The narrator tells us that Ked and Louisa, who was then

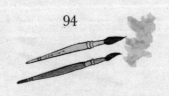

a famous fashion model, were lovers and then best friends, and that their friendship stayed strong across the decades. When Louisa asked Ked to headline a music festival held to save Millford's local libraries, he just couldn't say no, and came out of retirement specially.

There's a shot of Ked in the 1960s, sitting cross-legged in the park, reading a book while Louisa, wearing a minidress, white lipstick and spider-like false lashes, stands barefoot behind him, making a daisy chain.

'So cool,' Bex breathes.

And then the documentary proper begins, with Ked Wilder waking up, stretching, checking his alarm clock. The camera follows him as he makes a fruit smoothie for breakfast, strums a few chords on his guitar and jumps into a 1960s vintage Triumph Spitfire sports car and takes to the open road. He chats away to the camera as he drives, explaining that he can't wait to see his good friend Louisa and how this festival is worth coming out of retirement for.

Lexie sits beside me on the threadbare carpet, her face shining, eyes bright.

'This is awesome,' she whispers as the footage cuts to Ked arriving in Millford, throwing his arms round Louisa,

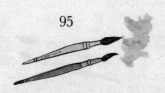

the two of them walking down through the grounds at Greystones and on into the festival itself. Louisa is telling him about us, the local kids who formed a band and want to save the libraries, and Ked says that music still has the power to change the world if only we believe it.

'Ked always speaks so well,' Ms Winter says fondly. 'Buckets of charm. Star quality, we used to call it – he's still got it!'

I glance at Marley who is wide-eyed, transfixed by the TV, probably wondering if he has star quality too.

'It's us!' Sasha yells abruptly as the camera tracks Ked and Louisa into the festival green room, which is actually just a glorified marquee. We see ourselves in the background, a huddle of anxious teens lurking beside the refreshments table. We're dressed as pirates in solidarity with Marley, who had been fighting the night before and had a black eye; Sasha had done a camouflage make-up job and even added a pirate eye patch for good measure.

'We look OK,' Lee declares.

'We look amazing!' Marley corrects him. 'This could be such great publicity for us. We need to find it online and copy the link and share it everywhere . . .'

'Shhhh!' everyone hisses, and the camera closes in on

Ked and Louisa talking about libraries to Lexie, Bex and Happi, and then moves to Marley, Lee and Sasha talking about the Lost & Found. I scan the screen and see myself, trying to blend into the background as usual and failing miserably. I am too tall, too scruffy to be in any way invisible. My hair is such a bird's nest I almost expect to see a couple of sparrows perched on it, and the overcoat . . . well, I can see how ratty it looks.

I can see why Marley hates it, and Aunt Zenna and Mr Simpson the head teacher. I can see why people laugh at it and make snarky comments. Lexie slides a hand into mine and squeezes, as if to tell me that she likes me anyway, scruff or not.

The camera zooms in on a shot of Sasha onstage, her sweet, clear voice singing the lyrics to the 'Library Song', and as the shot pulls back we get to see ourselves properly, up there on a festival stage, owning that stage, owning the crowd, the song a perfect slice of raw emotion and library love. We're good . . . really good. We work together as if instinctively, make it all look natural and easy.

I wish my family could see this. They'd be proud of me, I know they would.

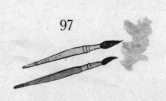

But this was filmed a month ago . . . and since then the band has fallen apart.

It's hard to imagine us being able to limp through even one song, let alone the set we aced at the festival. Glancing at Marley, I know he can see this too; this footage is a powerful reminder of how far we'd come and also how far we've let things slip.

The footage switches to Ked Wilder's set, a study in joyful, upbeat sixties pop, and then a final interview in which Ked implores Millford Council to keep the libraries open, and tells viewers to watch out for the Lost & Found's meteoric rise to fame.

'We underestimate kids these days,' he says. 'We write them off as lazy, feckless, waiting for us to hand them the world on a plate. Well, I'm here to tell you that we've got it all wrong – these kids, the Lost & Found, are proof of that. Twelve teenagers who've only been playing together for a matter of weeks have held us all spellbound with their talent, energy and sheer determination, and that's something I haven't seen in quite a while. I'll be keeping in touch with these kids, helping them as much as I can – I'd love to help them get into the recording studio, help bring some of these powerful, original songs of theirs to a wider audience!'

'Wow,' Lexie breathes, at my side. 'He really does believe in us!'

'Well, he would if he wasn't stuck in Provence,' Marley mutters.

On screen, Ked Wilder puts on his black fedora and pulls the brim down, laughing. 'Mark my words,' he says. 'These kids have something very special. Remember the name – the Lost & Found. This won't be the last time you hear it! And now that I've ventured out of retirement to have some fun with old friends and new ones, it won't be the last you hear of me either!'

The camera cuts to a shot of Ked giving Louisa one last hug before sliding into the driving seat of his Triumph Spitfire and waving from the window as he drives into the sunset.

'Goodness,' Ms Winter says, dabbing her eyes with what looks like a paint rag. 'He's wonderful, isn't he? And what a great showcase for you all!'

'We're famous!' Lexie grins. 'Thank you, Ms Winter, for telling us it was on – and letting us watch together! It was amazing!'

'It was!' the old lady agrees. 'It really was!'

I stack up the empty glasses and take them through to the big, old-fashioned kitchen, and Ms Winter follows with the empty lemonade jug and the remains of the chocolate digestives.

'Thank you, Sami,' she says. 'You and Lexie must pop in one day soon – there are a couple of things I wanted to ask you about. I'll make more lemonade, maybe even some cake . . .'

'That sounds good,' I say politely, wondering why Lexie and I are the only ones to get an extra invite. 'I'll tell her.'

'You do that!'

I say goodbye and join the others, heading for home through the darkened grounds of Greystones.

'That was incredible,' Bex says. 'Inspiring!'

'No,' Marley growls. 'That was a wake-up call.'

For once, I think I agree with Marley.

The fighting worsened. Men spoke of barrel bombs and torture and a leader who had turned against his people. Young men joined resistance groups to fight back.

There was talk of extremist groups too, bands of fighters who wanted to turn Syria into a different place completely, somewhere with no possibility of freedom or truth or silver linings. It was becoming difficult to know who the real enemy was. Danger was everywhere.

I sat at the dinner table sketching imaginary war scenes, pen and ink images of the grand city buildings of Damascus, scarred and crumbling, with tanks rolling along the streets.

'Don't draw such things!' my mother scolded, as if doing so would bring the fighting closer, but I'd seen the TV news, the pictures in the papers. I knew it was coming. I knew it was just a matter of time.

'The world will see what is happening,' my father said, tuning his radio to a European station to see if the west had come up with a solution for what was happening around us. 'They will help us. They will not stand by and let us die.'

My mother pressed her lips together and went on stitching, but now she wasn't sewing jackets or coats or party dresses, just darning a cardigan for my little sister and patching an old shirt I had almost grown out of.

'If it gets bad, we will go to my brother in Latakia,' my father said. Uncle Kawar and Aunt Sara lived in the north, in a seaside resort not far from the Turkish border. They would take us in if need be.

'If it gets bad, we will go to my brother Dara in London,' my mother argued. 'We may have to — for the sake of the children. I was born in Britain — I have citizenship. We would be safe there.'

That's when I knew things were serious, because I never thought I would hear my mother talk of leaving her beloved Syria.

'It won't come to that,' my father said, but my mother just sighed and kept sewing. I could see she did not share my father's faith that the world would step in and rescue us.

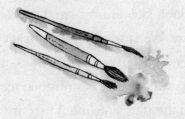

10

The Notebook

By the weekend, Lexie and I have worked our way through half of the dates list. As well as the park picnic, we've eaten chips wrapped in white paper, fed the ducks with a paper bag of cornmeal that cost 10p from the park visitor centre, drunk iced coffees in the Leaping Llama, been to the cinema (a Disney film) and now we are wandering around the art gallery in town.

After the last few years, it seems amazing and wonderful to do such simple things and find happiness in them. I thought I had forgotten how, but Lexie helps me to see that isn't so.

We look at piles of rusty scrap metal and wall-sized

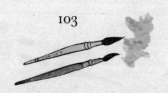

canvases that look like an over-sized toddler has flung his dinner at them. We study bright abstract images where every face seems to have several noses, an extra eye, a grimacing mouth filled with tombstone teeth. I don't like all of them, but they fascinate me. There are about a million ways to make sense of the world, but art is probably the most awesome.

We find Louisa Winter's famous painting of a sad-eyed woman holding a fox at the top of a staircase, and although it is very different from anything else I've ever seen, I love it. Ms Winter is Millford's most famous artist, but somehow it's hard to link this powerful canvas with the eccentric elderly lady with paintbrushes in her hair who owns Greystones and hangs out with legendary 1960s pop stars.

Lexie seems mesmerized. 'It makes my head spin,' she says. 'Like I'm so, so close to understanding . . . well, life, the universe, everything. If I could just work out what the picture is trying to say to me! Does that sound crazy?'

'Not to me,' I tell her. 'It's a great painting. A part of you wants to understand it totally, and another part knows you never can . . .'

Lexie links an arm through mine.

'That's another one ticked off the dates list,' Lexie comments. 'It's a shame we're halfway through. What happens when we run out? Should we think up some new date ideas?'

'Definitely,' I agree. 'Lots of them! Hundreds. Thousands, maybe. Although, to be fair, I think I could sit in an empty room with you for hours on end and never get bored.'

'You say the sweetest things!' she teases. 'An empty room?'

'You know what I mean,' I argue. 'Thanks for coming here with me . . . I've loved it. The Louisa Winter painting is incredible. I knew she was a force of nature, but I had no clue how talented she is as an artist.'

'I know!' Lexie agrees. 'I hate to admit it, but I'd never even heard of her until Jake found us the old railway carriage to practise in. Weird, huh?'

We're walking hand in hand out of the gallery building when I spot a little heap of flyers on the information desk beside the exit. It's Louisa Winter's name that jumps out at me first, and then the mention of a refugee charity called Footsteps to Freedom.

My heart starts to race.

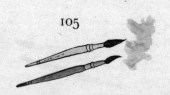

'Look,' I say to Lexie. 'Look at this!'

The flyer is advertising an exhibition of Louisa Winter's newest paintings, which will run from the start of October, with all proceeds going to help the refugee charity.

'Wow,' Lexie breathes. 'She really is awesome, isn't she?'

'No, Lexie, listen,' I say. 'This charity . . . I mean . . . I know them. They are amazing people. They helped me – they helped me so much. Without them, I would never have got to England!'

Once the words start tumbling out, I want to tell her everything – what happened in Greece, what happened afterwards, the coat, the fear, the hunger, the hopelessness. I want to explain that the charity Louisa Winter is fundraising for saved my life, but the words are stuck in my throat like shards of broken glass. Unexpectedly, my eyes flood with hot tears and I have to pull away. I let go of Lexie's hand, and the flyer falls crumpled to the floor.

I bite the inside of my cheek until it bleeds, drag the sleeve of my overcoat across my eyes. We're outside now, the sunshine bright, and Lexie knows somehow that I need space to get myself together, space to calm down. I sit cross-legged in the shade of a weeping willow and wonder

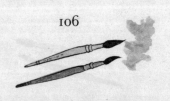

what it could be that makes a tree weep, ribbons of leaves falling down to the ground like tears.

Lexie heads to an ice-cream van with a long queue and buys two cornets with chocolate flakes and strawberry sauce. By the time she comes back, the past has receded again, like the ocean at low tide. I know it will come back . . . it always does.

'Ice cream from a proper British ice-cream van,' Lexie says, grinning. 'That's another one ticked off the list.

I am glad that Lexie is not the kind of girl to make a fuss, and that she understands that sometimes a tidal wave of pain can catch you unawares and almost pull you under. We are silent for a while, eating the sweet, cool ice cream.

'If you ever want to talk . . . well, I'll listen,' she says quietly. 'I won't tell anyone else, I promise.'

I shake my head. 'I can't,' I say, and my voice has dropped to a whisper. 'I can't talk about it. I wish I could. Too hard.'

I know that if I could talk to anyone about the past, anyone at all, it would be Lexie – but where would I start? With the sound of bombs and gunfire we heard every night from our house in Damascus? With a beach on Kos? A boy walking until the soles of his boots wore clean away? Images

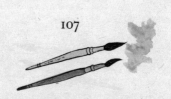

flash into my mind, each one twisting my heart with pain. Collecting ring pulls and silver paper from the roadside, playing the flute while Nazz and Joe ran along behind me, Amira dancing ahead in her ragged princess dress and broken fairy wings.

I push the memories away.

I would like someone to understand. I'd like Lexie to, and there is a way I can do that without saying a single word. My fingers shake as I slide the little notebook out of my pocket, hold it out to her.

'Um . . .' she says. 'Your drawings, right?'

But then she opens the book and sees it all – the writing, the sketches, the pain. Sometimes I think the pages must be stained with blood and salt water and tears, but they're not, of course.

The notebook was my social worker's idea; it's what I'm supposed to do with my thoughts, fears, memories. I can't talk about those things – the words lodge in my throat like a tangle of barbed wire. They cannot be spoken, but somehow I can sketch and write my memories in the pages of my notebook.

'I'm not asking you to share what you write with me,'

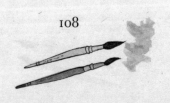

Ben had said. 'Not if you don't want to. I'm just asking you to acknowledge the past . . . If something comes to the surface, even if it's something painful, write it down. Let it out, Sami. OK?'

These days, when the past seeps into my bloodstream like poison, I find words and pictures to give it shape. Somehow, it lessens the ache. I write in English, because that is my language now; the words I grew up with, words in Kurdish and Arabic, belong to a different life.

I watch Lexie as she leafs through the notebook. Her fingers smooth the pages, reading a story that's so painful, so personal, I have kept it hidden from every other human being I know. There is the sketch of my mother's face, the drawing of the tented encampment on the Turkish border, the picture of the boat that sank in the Aegean. These words and images are my truth, my darkness.

I shut my eyes and let the shimmering ribbons of willow shade my skin, and when I open my eyes again Lexie is staring at me, her eyes brimming with tears.

'No words,' she whispers, and she puts her arms around me, presses her cheek against mine, beneath the willow tree in the bright August sunshine.

My father put down the letter with tears in his eyes. I had never seen my father cry; he was tall, he was strong, he always knew what to do.

'What is it?' I asked. 'What's wrong?'

'This damn war!' he burst out. 'This damn war! What is a man to do?'

The letter was from my father's best friend, a teacher in Aleppo, telling us that he had lost his sons in a barrel-bomb attack. The fighting was here in Damascus too; my father's cousin had vanished one evening walking home from the market and nobody knew what had happened to him.

'Samir, I want you and Roza at home from now on,' my father said. 'No more school. The streets are too dangerous. You can do your lessons here, and help in the shop . . .'

Anger bubbled up inside me. I liked school . . . I was good at my lessons, and the teachers said I had a talent for drawing and music.

I didn't want to be stuck in the shop every day with nobody but my family for company.

'That's not fair!' I burst out. 'What about my friends?'

My father wiped his eyes and stood tall again, his arms folded. 'No more school,' he said.

And then a barrel bomb exploded in the next street, and my friend Azif was killed. I'd known him since our first day at school, played football with him, learned to play the flute with him. He knew that I liked halva and lemon-drop sweets and hated the taste of Coca-Cola; he knew he could beat me at running, that I liked being in goal when we played football, that I wanted to be an artist when I grew up.

'We'll go to university together,' he'd told me, once. 'You can train to be an artist and I'll train to be a lawyer. It'll be cool!'

We would never do that now, of course. We would never do anything together again.

I sat up late into the night, listening to my father and mother discuss the future. Should we stay? Should we go? They argued and debated as the city emptied and our friends and neighbours began to head for the borders.

'We must leave,' my father said. 'It is more dangerous day by day. There will be nobody to rescue us — the rest of the world does not care.'

My mother started to cry. 'Oh, Karim, I am afraid. This is still my home . . . and who is to say that leaving will not be more dangerous than staying? I do not want to go.'

'We have no choice,' he told her.

11

Pretty Street

Nobody in the whole wide world knows more about me now than Lexie Lawlor. It's a terrifying thought but an exhilarating one too.

My shoulders feel lighter, stronger, as if someone has lifted away a rucksack full of pain that I've been carrying for way too long. I remember the rucksack I carried on my journey . . . I remember packing it, the day we left home to travel north to my father's brother in Latakia, near the Turkish border.

'Pack only the essentials,' my father had said. 'When we get to London, we will start again. There, everything will be better!'

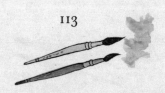

I remember my mother's eyes, defeated even then, and I'd made sure to pack my hopes and dreams into that rucksack along with the shirts, the T-shirts, the warm jumper. I packed my flute too, slung across my body in a plastic case inside a canvas carrier. My sister Roza wore her best party dress, the colour of the ocean, and my mother wore the emerald-green scarf with the rose print and the silky fringing that my father had bought for her on her last birthday. My father was smart and formal in a tweed overcoat with a grey satin lining that he'd tailored himself. I put on my best pair of boots and a new padded jacket, even though the weather was warm, and I hauled the rucksack on to my back.

I lost that rucksack in the sea, but the flute survived and the aid workers gave me a new rucksack. As my journey went on, it grew heavier and heavier; I acquired a sleeping bag, a small tent, a new pair of boots. I think it was the pain, though, that really weighed my rucksack down. It may have been invisible, but the weight of it almost broke me, and even when I set my rucksack down for the final time, on the shiny laminate floor of my aunt and uncle's flat in Millford, the weight of that pain pressed down on me still.

I thought I would carry it forever, but when I handed Lexie my notebook yesterday, something shifted. It feels like someone else is helping to carry the burden now, for a while at least.

Marley calls an all-band meeting in the Leaping Llama to announce his plan to get the Lost & Found back on track. It's not what anyone expects.

'Covers,' he declares, sipping frappuccino from a jam-jar glass. 'That's what we need. A rock-solid catalogue of top-quality covers to educate us about how the legends did it . . .'

'Covers?' I say to Lexie, thinking of quilts and blankets and wondering how they could possibly help our playing. 'I don't get it!'

'That's what they call it when you play someone else's song,' she explains.

'Oh . . .'

Marley has always been against playing other people's songs on principle, but now that he and Lexie are no longer dating their songwriting output has plunged to zero. With inspiration at an all-time low and a tone-deaf keyboardist

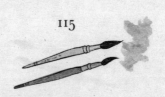

to work around, we definitely need something to give us a jump-start.

'We're getting stale,' Marley decrees. 'Messing things up that we should know inside out. The pressure's off and we've let ourselves drift, and that's bad news. I've been reading this library book about how Ked Wilder made the big time – and there's no magic formula. He puts it down to practice, pure and simple. It makes sense, right? The more you practise, the better you get.'

He frowns at Bobbi-Jo, who seems to be the exception to this rule, then ploughs on.

'Ked Wilder played a gig a day for an entire year, apparently, and lots of the songs he played were covers. He reckons he learned all he needed to know about songwriting from playing those covers . . . like a kind of masterclass in lyrics and melodies and hooks.'

'Hooks?' Bobbi-Jo echoes, fiddling with her straw. 'What are you talking about?'

'A song's hook is the catchy bit that gets you singing along,' Jake tells her. 'The bit that fixes itself in your head and gets you humming the tune.'

'I knew that,' Bobbi-Jo sniffs. 'Obviously.'

'So we learn ten new songs,' Marley continues. 'I've chosen ten summer classics, each with something different to teach us, each hugely popular and successful. The discipline will be good for us, and if we pick up any gigs over the next few weeks we can slip a few in along with our originals to bring our set up to the right length. OK?'

'Sounds good,' Lee says. 'I agree, we need something to kick us out of our comfort zone. Any plans to get us some gigs?'

'Not yet,' Marley admits. 'But Bobbi-Jo and I have some plans in the pipeline. We'll keep you posted once we know more, but if things work out as hoped . . . Well, put it this way, getting gigs won't be a problem.'

'*Bobbi-Jo and I have some plans?*' Bex repeats. 'You're making plans without telling the rest of us? I thought we were a team?'

'Oh, for goodness' sake!' Bobbi-Jo snaps. 'You're so touchy! Does everything have to be a team decision? Like what shoes I'm going to wear tomorrow? What I should have for my tea? We're doing this for the band and as soon as there's anything to tell, you'll know!'

'Er . . . what Bobbi-Jo said,' Marley echoes. 'Sort of . . .'

Bex looks mutinous and the row seems likely to escalate, but at that moment three teenagers swagger over to the table. They look a bit like kids dressed up for a fancy-dress party, with low-slung black Levis, white hi-tops and baseball caps worn backwards. The skinniest, spottiest guy, who is wearing a new denim jacket with a Run-DMC patch, pulls a few bizarre hand gestures and offers his palm to Marley for a high five. Marley, looking totally confused, sticks his hand in the air and allows it to be slapped.

'Cool to meet you, man,' the kid says in a broad Brummie accent. 'Marley, right? And you must all be the Lost & Found.'

'Er – yes,' Marley says.

'I'm T-Dawg,' the boy explains. 'I've heard a lot about you, and I expect you've heard about us; we're Pretty Street!'

Marley tries not to smirk. 'The rap band? Seriously?'

'Oh, we're serious all right,' T-Dawg says. 'We're Millford's answer to Eminem. Or Stormzy, maybe. So we just wanted to borrow Bobbi-Jo for a little while, OK? We're old friends, aren't we? Go back a long way. And we wanted to ask some advice – can you spare a minute, Bobbi-Jo? If that's OK with the rest of you?'

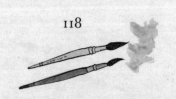

'Cool,' Bobbi-Jo says, pink-faced and smiling.

'Go right ahead,' Bex adds generously. 'You're welcome!'

Bobbi-Jo gets up, wriggles out of the booth and follows T-Dawg and his friends over to a distant table.

'Advice?' Marley echoes, as they depart.

'On style, maybe?' Bex quips.

'T-Dawg is *so* not how I imagined him,' Lexie says, and we sit in silence for a moment, trying not to laugh.

'He's only borrowed Bobbi-Jo,' Bex whispers wickedly. 'Think we could get him to keep her?

We packed our bags, ready to travel; that was one of the hardest things of all. How do you choose what to leave behind? How do you pare your life down to the basics, walk away from the things that have meant so much for so long? My father took letters and photographs, my mother took the quilt she had stitched before her marriage, my little sister packed her favourite toys — but it wasn't about possessions, not really. Walking away from the house that had been home for so long . . . that was the hardest thing.

We drove to Latakia, where my father's brother Kawar lived with his family. The plan was for all of us to travel to the border and on into Turkey, and I tried to pretend that we were on holiday, visiting the cousins, looking forward to days at the beach with ice cream and paddleboards and laughter, like so many holidays that had gone before. That was the story we stuck to when we were stopped by roadblocks every few miles, quizzed by different factions and warned to stay off the roads for our own safety.

We made it to Latakia, tired and scared, sticky from the heat, parched from the dust. Uncle Kawar told us he'd changed his mind about leaving; Aunt Sara was expecting another baby. The journey would be too dangerous, too tiring for her now, and what kind of life could they expect at the other end?

'A free one,' my father said, but Uncle Kawar wasn't so sure. We left the car with them, and Uncle Kawar said that if we needed funds at any point he would sell it and wire us the money. He wished us luck, and we wished him luck, and then everyone hugged goodbye. My family caught a bus to the Turkish border. Our journey had begun.

12

Today Millford, Tomorrow the World

'Guess what?' Bobbi-Jo says at practice a few days later. 'I've got the most amazing news! Will you tell them, Marley, or shall I?'

Marley sighs. 'Go right ahead.'

'We're going to be famous!' she crows. 'We're going to be on the radio and win a day's free recording in a proper studio, find ourselves a manager, maybe even have a number-one hit!'

We're all gathered in the old railway carriage ready to practise, but nobody looks especially thrilled at Bobbi-Jo's news.

'Who told you this?' Bex asks, tuning her bass guitar.

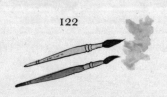

'Was it the tooth fairy? Santa Claus? A talking faun with Turkish Delight who came from a land where it's always winter and never Christmas?'

'Huh?' Bobbi-Jo huffs. 'I don't actually know what you're talking about, Bex, and I don't think you do either. Look, I was talking to my dad about the Lost & Found and how few openings there are for new bands these days, and he came up with a brilliant idea to help us. A Battle of the Bands competition! The radio station love the idea – they want to invite local bands to perform live on radio over a period of two weeks . . . and get listeners ringing in to vote, like Eurovision or something. How cool? And Dad's called in a favour from a friend who owns a recording studio in Birmingham, and he's giving a day's recording time as the prize. I mean, this competition is totally made for us, right?'

Bex raises an eyebrow. 'The fact that your dad works for the radio station isn't going to look just a tiny bit suspicious if we win then?'

Bobbi-Jo scowls. 'You're always so negative!' she grumbles. 'The people of Millford will choose the winner. Dad'll be totally impartial, obviously, but if he really, really likes the sound of the winning band, he might take them on as manager. He misses that side of the music business, I think.'

Lexie and I exchange glances. 'Wow,' I say. 'You're saying we might end up recording a single – and getting a manager too?'

'What about Ked Wilder?' Happi asks. 'He's supposed to be our mentor – shouldn't we run those kind of decisions past him?'

'How do we do that, exactly?' Marley challenges. 'Ked's great, but he's off the radar right now. We can't afford to wait around forever, and this competition is exactly what we need to get focused again. We don't have much competition locally, do we? We'll smash it!'

'Modesty has always been your most attractive trait, Marley,' Bex says, and he shrugs.

'Look, this hasn't been advertised yet,' he says. 'Bobbi-Jo and her dad have come up with the idea together, and I for one am grateful. It's the first time Millford has done anything like this, and I really do think we can win!'

'Of course we can,' Bobbi-Jo says. 'There's practically no opposition!'

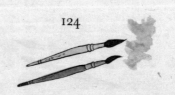

'There's Pretty Street,' Bex says, grinning. 'Friends of yours, I believe?'

Bobbi-Jo shrugs. 'I've known T-Dawg since I was five years old. He wasn't T-Dawg then, he was Thomas Dawes. He's had a crush on me since reception class . . . Are you jealous, Marley?'

'Why would I be?' Marley asks. 'You're with us, not them. Aren't you?'

'Well, obviously,' she says. 'They were just asking for advice on dance moves yesterday. I'm fully trained, you know – street dance, jazz, tap, ballet . . .'

'You're teaching them to pirouette?' Lee sniggers.

'Don't be ridiculous. I'm just giving them some tips on how to move and how to stand. Don't laugh – we could do with thinking about that sort of thing too. You can't just stand there like a limp dishrag when you're on stage in front of thousands, you know!'

'We managed OK at the festival,' Marley points out.

'Yes, but it could have been so much better – Romy and Lexie should be bopping about as they do the backing vocals, and Sasha could do some subtle twerking . . .'

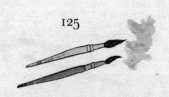

'Is there such a thing?' Sasha asks, alarmed. 'Even if there is – no way!'

'Well, I'm just saying, don't underestimate Pretty Street,' Bobbi-Jo says. 'They're serious about what they do, and once they find out about the Battle of the Bands they'll definitely be signing up.'

'They're a joke,' Marley says dismissively. 'No threat to us. Who else might enter?'

'Plenty,' Jake says. 'My stepdad plays with a local ceilidh band – they might go for it. There's a bunch of middle-aged lorry drivers in pork-pie hats who play ska tunes – and don't forget Zombie Massacre. All kinds of people are making music in Millford.'

'Enough chat,' he says. 'We've got to up our game – end of story. Right, let's practise. Let's start with the summer playlist – and I want it perfect. We've got to nail this!'

Half an hour in, my head is hurting from the noise, and Marley's not looking impressed either. 'No, no, keep it simple,' he yells yet again, waving his arms to halt proceedings. 'Bobbi-Jo, focus on getting the notes right. You said you'd practise!'

'I have practised!' she argues. 'Maybe it's Sasha's singing that's off? Or Lexie's backing vocals?'

'It's the keyboards,' Marley says firmly. 'I'm sorry, Bobbi-Jo, you're playing a bunch of notes that shouldn't be there.'

'I'm just doing what you showed me,' she says, crestfallen, and I can't help feeling a bit sorry for her then. 'Maybe you showed me wrong? Should we have some more one-to-one practices, so I know for sure?'

'I suppose so,' Marley says with a sigh. 'I've already simplified the keyboard parts as much as I can. I've pared them right back to a simple two-note beat, but it's still not working. A few more days' practice, I guess . . .'

'Is he kidding?' Lee says under his breath. 'Never mind a few days, a few decades wouldn't be long enough. She can't play!'

The practice disintegrates. Lee, George and Jake are playing card games, Bex unplugs her bass and starts reading *The Fault in Our Stars*, and I abandon the flute to sketch my band mates on the back of some discarded sheet music. Eventually, Marley calls it a day and people start to head off.

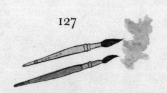

'You still haven't told her you're gay,' Lexie says to Marley as we watch Bobbi-Jo walk across the grass, blowing him a kiss over her shoulder. 'That's rotten, Marley – we can all see she fancies you.'

'I'll tell her soon,' he argues. 'I just don't want to hurt her feelings. She really is trying, and her dad's a great contact – we can win this competition and show him we're a band worth taking on. Today Millford, tomorrow the world!'

I still have nightmares about the camp in Turkey. It was a crazy shanty town of dirty canvas tents, crammed with people, loud with shouting, screaming, singing, sobbing. Every day, a truck would come with sacks of rice and beans; you had to queue to get a ration, and water came from a rusty standpipe with a puddle beneath it.

We were out of Syria, but this didn't feel like freedom. It felt like chaos.

There were too many people squashed in together, packed tight like animals on the way to market and just as scared. There was kindness and camaraderie, but also greed and spite and avarice, and plenty of people trying to make some cash from the misfortunes of others. There was sickness too, an invisible fog that swirled around us.

'This isn't good, Karim,' my mother said. 'We're not safe here. We're hungry every day. How long before the children get sick? Did we leave our home for this?'

'Of course not,' my father replied. 'This is just a stopgap. Things will be better once we get to Europe.'

That same day, a gang of older kids attacked me near the wash-tents and stole my new padded jacket and the parcel of rice and beans I was taking back to the tent. When my father saw the bruises blooming like dark poison all over my body, black and blue and violet, he made his decision.

We would walk to freedom, starting the very next day.

13

In the Artist's Studio

The first time Lexie comes to tea at our flat, my aunt and uncle practically roll out a red carpet.

'Welcome!' Aunt Zenna says, beaming at her. 'Welcome to our home! You are the girl who has made our Sami tidy himself up, comb his hair occasionally! You have put a smile on his face once more!'

'Have I?' Lexie asks, looking slightly overwhelmed. 'Well . . . that's good! He's put a smile on my face too!'

My uncle insists on conducting a guided tour of the workshop, and flicking through a family photo album showing my cousins Taz and Faizah at various ages, in school uniform, graduating from uni, and, in Faizah's case,

getting married. Lexie manages to make all the right noises, and even admires a slightly scary picture of Faizah's toddler son with ice cream all over his face.

Aunt Zenna has produced a Syrian feast, and Lexie tries everything.

'I am getting to love Syrian food!' she exclaims. 'Hummus and lebna with za'atar and ful . . . they're great! Beats pizza and chips any day!'

'Oh, we love pizza and chips too,' my aunt confesses. 'But I thought you'd appreciate something traditional, something special!'

'I do!' Lexie says, and my aunt and uncle have to visibly restrain themselves from throwing their arms around her. Lexie's goodness shines out of her, it seems, and I'm not the only one to see it.

'So, where is our nephew taking you tonight?' my uncle asks Lexie.

'Stargazing,' she says. 'That's all I know, but I bet it'll be fun!'

My aunt frowns. 'Sami, no,' she protests. 'Not the fire escape! It's an eyesore! That's no kind of a date for a lovely young lady like Lexie!'

But that's where we go, all the same, Lexie laughing and Uncle Dara shaking his head in despair and Aunt Zenna offering to make us a flask of her hot sweet coffee.

'Your aunt and uncle are so lovely!' Lexie tells me as I spread a blanket for us to sit on. 'They think the world of you!'

'They think I'm mad,' I say. 'But I reckon they see you as a good influence. You'd better stick with me!'

'I'll think about it,' she says, grinning.

According to the internet, there are supposed to be meteor showers tonight, but all we can see is the fuzzy orange glow from Millford's street lights. Meteor showers and falling stars might be happening right now above our heads, and we'd never even know it.

That's sort of sad, but still, it's good to have someone to sit with once more beneath the night sky, and a fuzzy orange glow is better than the flash and roar of the bombs that lit up the skies of Syria in those weeks before we left.

I take Lexie's hand in the darkness.

'I'm not sure the Lost & Found are actually going to win

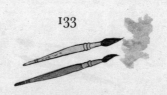

this competition,' she muses after a while. 'Not unless Bobbi-Jo's playing improves. We're on very rocky ground!'

'Try telling Marley that,' I say. 'He's so obsessed that he won't listen to any criticism at all! I don't think this will end well.'

'Nope,' Lexie agrees, squinting skyward. 'Does this date count as stargazing if we don't see any stars?'

'They're up there,' I promise. 'Somewhere . . .'

'Bex has a poster on her bedroom wall with an Oscar Wilde quote on it,' Lexie says. ' "We are all in the gutter, but some of us are looking at the stars," it says. Something like that, anyway.'

'We're on the fire escape, not in the gutter,' I say.

'Same thing,' she says.

'Bike ride tomorrow,' I remind her. 'That's almost the last thing on the dates list – we'll need to make a new one. Meet at eleven in the park? You can give me a guided tour of Millford on two wheels!'

'You managed to borrow one then?' Lexie asks.

'From the charity shop next door,' I admit. 'They said I could take it for a test ride in exchange for helping them in the shop one morning. It's years since I've ridden a bike!'

'It's something you don't forget,' Lexie points out. 'It'll be fun, I promise. Sami, do you want to know something? Something weird, something sad? Something I've never told anyone else?'

I frown. 'Sure,' I say. 'If you want to tell me.'

She settles into the curve of my arm. 'You might think I'm stupid . . .'

'You're not stupid,' I tell her. 'I'd never think that.'

Lexie sighs. 'It's about my mum. I still miss her loads, y'know. For a long time I had stuff I wanted to tell her, stuff I needed to ask her . . . and she wasn't here to ask. So after she left, I used to write her letters. At first, I sent them to the flat we used to live in, but the social worker told me to stop. The new people were getting kind of freaked out. I kept writing anyway, but I had nowhere to send the letters, so I'd slip a note into the pages of a library book, fold one into the shape of a paper boat and launch it on the park lake, drop one into the flames of a bonfire. I thought that somehow my mum might get the message.'

'Oh, Lexie . . .'

'I did it until a few weeks ago,' she says. 'Crazy, huh? It's hard to let go of the past.'

135

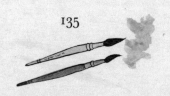

'It's not crazy,' I say. 'It's human. It's actually kind of lovely. I'd give anything to be able to say goodbye to my family. I still have my father's mobile phone – it doesn't work, of course. The charger is long gone, but what wouldn't I give to fire it up and call his number, hear his voice one last time . . .'

'Why don't you?' Lexie says. 'Just get a new charger. You can get all kinds of old kit on the internet. It wouldn't be hard to find the right one, I bet!'

I blink. 'You think it would still work? After all this time?'

Lexie shrugs. 'Maybe. Worth a try, surely? You could leave a message. A sort of goodbye voicemail . . . a mobile-phone version of the letters I used to send.'

'Yeah,' I say. 'Maybe I could!'

'It might help,' she tells me. 'In some strange way, it might help you let go.'

The thought of letting go, saying goodbye, is a tangle of love and grief in my soul. It would mean accepting that my family are gone, but maybe I need to do that before I can get on with my own life.

There are so many things I want to say to them, though. I know that I have to try, even if it's painful.

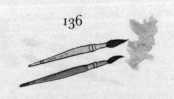

I lean my head back against the rusty fire escape and gaze at the sky, thinking of the roof garden back home in Damascus. I don't even know if our home is still standing; I think the stars shine above a ruined city now.

There are no shooting stars here tonight, not for us, but just being with Lexie is pretty much perfect. Besides, I have a contingency plan. I take a Coke-can star from my pocket and hand it to her, and she smiles and snuggles closer.

The next day, I give Aunt Zenna a swift hug as I head out of the door, coat-tails flapping, to collect the bicycle from next door. It's a big, old-fashioned thing, and only a little bit rusty in places, which is more than can be said for me. I sit astride it, suddenly uncertain.

'Good luck, Sami!' says Mr Jones, the manager of the charity shop, and I grin and push off from the kerb, wobbling all the way along the street.

By the time I get to the park, the bike seems less unwieldy. I am flying along, my coat fluttering in the breeze, an older version of the eight-year-old kid who once spent weekends constructing cross-country bike tracks with his friends in the hills just beyond the city.

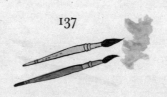

I meet Lexie at the park cafe and the two of us set off on our tour: a circuit of Millford and a detour into the countryside. We stop a couple of hours later to share a sandwich in the park, then wheel our bikes towards Greystones with the plan of calling on Louisa Winter.

'Do I look like I've been sleeping under a bridge?' I ask Lexie, remembering one of Aunt Zenna's accusation from a couple of months ago.

'No. Why, have you?' she retorts.

'Not recently,' I say. 'My aunt reckons I'm a scruff. She's determined to get me to ditch the coat and get a haircut.'

'The coat's seen better days, but so what?' Lexie says with a shrug. 'It has character. And the hair . . . I love it just the way it is!'

I wonder if Aunt Zenna would like Lexie quite as much if she heard that.

As we pass the old railway carriage, we can hear the cats-being-strangled racket of Bobbi-Jo having an extra keyboard lesson. 'She's improving,' Lexie says, and I have to laugh, because I don't think it's actually possible for Bobbi-Jo to be any worse.

I rake a hand through my hair in a futile attempt to tidy

myself up as we walk up the stone steps to the front door at Greystones, and Lexie rings the bell. There's a long silence, and then the door creaks open and there is Louisa Winter, red hair tumbling over a paint-stained apron, a paint palette still in her hand.

'Children!' she says, opening the door wide, as if she was expecting us at exactly this moment. 'How lovely! Come in! I have chocolate brownies, and pink lemonade in the fridge. Come through to the studio and I'll fetch them!'

We walk along an old-fashioned hallway to the back of the house, where we are ushered into the studio, a big room with high ceilings and huge sash windows that flood the space with natural light. Three easels hold paintings at various stages of completion, and dozens more canvases are stacked against the walls. Each painting is breathtaking, depicting stark, stylized figures and animals that seem to hint at a meaning far darker, more magical than the obvious. The images draw you in, make you feel still and silent and awed.

I could stay here forever, breathing in the smell of oil paint and turps and linseed oil, my eyes skimming the table crowded with half-used tubes of paint, palettes and jars of brushes, taking in the paint-stained sofas, the dressing screens, the giant tribal shield, the hat stand draped with huge swathes of jewel-bright silk and velvet.

'Wow,' I say, because there are no words to describe this; no words in any language. 'Just . . . wow!'

'D'you like it?' Ms Winter asks, coming in with a pitcher of pink lemonade with ice and strawberry halves, and the promised plate of brownies. I just nod, my eyes burning, because I have never seen anything like this before, never imagined that art could hold so much power.

'It's amazing,' I say at last, turning to face her. I know my face must be bright with the thrill of it – childish, joyful – but I don't care. Something has been switched on inside me, a little flame of hope.

Lexie slips her hand into mine.

'Sami's an artist too,' she says. 'His drawings are amazing!'

'Not really,' I say, but Ms Winter smiles and says she saw the birthday card I made for Romy, and that she thinks I have talent.

'You have to believe, Sami,' she tells me. 'You have to care – you have to have something to say. That's what art is all about!'

'I think so too,' I say.

140

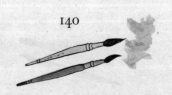

'We saw the flyer for your exhibition at the art gallery in town,' Lexie is saying. 'It looks fantastic!'

'What's going on in the Middle East and Europe is perhaps the biggest humanitarian crisis of our time,' Ms Winter says. 'It's huge, and yet we turn our faces away and pretend it isn't happening. Well, it is happening – you know that better than anyone, Sami – and it won't go away just because we'd like it to. I've had a good life, you know, but this . . . it keeps me awake at night. I want to help, and the only thing I could think of was to do something art-related . . . a sort of retrospective exhibition.'

'With all the profits going to Footsteps to Freedom,' Lexie says. 'That's awesome. I mean, just one of your paintings must be worth hundreds of pounds!'

'Thousands, actually,' Ms Winter says thoughtfully, pouring out tall glasses of lemonade. 'One sold for sixty thousand last year. People seem to like them; I really don't know why. The art world can be very fickle. But my agent has been asking me for some time now to put something together, old work and new, and this gives me the chance to do that. At least the exhibition will do something good, something practical.'

'It really will,' Lexie agrees.

'Thank you for what you are doing,' I say. 'Footsteps to Freedom is the charity that helped to bring me to Britain. Without them, I don't know what would have happened to me.'

'Oh, Sami, that's amazing!' Ms Winter says. 'I have to admit I first contacted them after meeting you at the library protest. I don't know your story, of course, but there are so many young people just like you – lost, displaced, running from countries torn apart by war or famine. They didn't ask for any of this. Perhaps, like you, they have lost their families. Footsteps to Freedom helps those children. It's such a good cause!'

She sighs, sliding chocolate brownies on to little side plates that are probably antiques. 'Sit down, sit down, please.'

We perch awkwardly on the paint-stained sofa, clutching the ice-cold lemonade and the cake.

'The thing is,' Ms Winter continues, 'I'm going to need your help. This exhibition isn't just about raising money – it's about raising awareness too. I'm planning a private view to start things off, and I thought that if the band could play

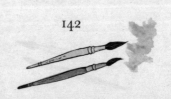

in the foyer of the gallery, perhaps, that would be wonderful! I can pay a small fee, but I know you'll have to ask the others.'

'We'll do it,' I say.

'No problem,' Lexie agrees. 'And no fee. It's for charity!'

I squeeze Lexie's hand, smiling. She knows how much this means to me, of course. I'd do anything in my power to support Footsteps to Freedom, to raise money, raise awareness. Playing at the private view is the very least we can do.

'We might even be able to work on a new song,' Lexie says, glancing at me. 'If Sami wants to . . .'

'I want to,' I say. 'That's a great idea!'

'Sometimes,' she says, 'A song can do amazing things. Move mountains, change opinions, open hearts – make people care. I think a song can make people care better than almost anything else in the world.'

'Oh, how wonderful!' Ms Winter exclaims. 'I can't imagine writing about it all would be easy, but if you could . . . well, I'd love that. You've already done so much, Sami. You really have had an impact on the local community – opened our eyes, made us see!'

'Oh, OK,' I say. 'That's . . . good. I think!'

We drink the pink lemonade and eat the brownies and thank Ms Winter for what she is doing, and it's only when we're in the hallway again, about to leave, that she drops her bombshell.

'There is one last favour I'd like to ask of you, Sami,' she says. 'It's not something I do very much any more. I tend to work mostly from my imagination now, but in this case I think it would give a real focus to the exhibition . . .'

'What would?' I ask.

'I'd like to paint you, Sami,' she says.

'What's a people smuggler?' my little sister Roza asked. 'I don't understand.'

'I don't understand either,' I told her. 'I don't know whether they are bad people, or brave people, or just plain greedy people . . . but if they can help us get to Europe, I don't suppose that matters.'

We were in Bodrum, a city on the Turkish coast just a few miles from the Greek island of Kos. For a fee, the smugglers would take us across the water to Europe; we were to meet at a small coastal village outside the city at 3 a.m. My father sealed our passports into individual plastic ziplock bags to be worn inside our clothing. His passport was filled with photographs and letters and he put it with his mobile phone into a slim plastic box that snapped tight like a shell. He slid this into the inside pocket of his overcoat.

When we arrived at the meeting point, we were alarmed to find not the dozen or so fellow passengers we'd been led to expect, but fifty. 'Perhaps they have secured a bigger boat,' my father wondered, but when the boat appeared, bumping up against the quayside, it wasn't big at all. It was a small, open-decked fishing boat. Even the moonlight couldn't hide its peeling paint and rusted outboard motor, nor the glint of impatience in the eyes of its captain.

We had been promised life jackets, but there were not enough. Roza's was OK, but mine was so big it swamped me, and it had broken ties. I could swim well — every year when we went to Latakia I swam in the ocean and played on my uncle's surfboard. I gave the life jacket to my mother, and she looped the emerald-green scarf tightly around it and knotted it at her waist. I shivered in a thin jumper, my flute slung diagonally across my body, the rucksack on my shoulders. My father was at least warm in his tweed overcoat with the silver lining.

The boat was so low in the water that I could trail my hand across the icy waves. We were packed in like sardines in a can, women and children towards the front and men in the stern, standing, because there was no space for them to sit. The captain shouted that we had to be still, we had to be silent, that the slightest movement could capsize us. The sea was choppy and there was a brisk wind, which added to the risk. It was life or death, the captain told us, as if we didn't understand that already.

He gunned the engine and the overloaded boat moved slowly out from the quay.

14

The Muse

'You're going to be immortalized by a famous painter,' Lexie teases. 'My boyfriend, the artist's muse!'

I laugh, because I never imagined I would be anybody's boyfriend – yet here I am with my defrosted heart and all kinds of crazy ideas unfurling in my mind, ideas for a future I didn't think I cared about. It looks like I do, after all.

'I need to be at Greystones tomorrow at ten,' I say. 'What will my uncle say when I don't turn up at the workshop? What will my girlfriend say when I fail to appear with flowers or chocolate bars?'

'You never give me flowers!' Lexie declares, in mock outrage, and I swoop down and pick a red poppy from the long grass.

She puts it behind her ear and sticks her tongue out at me, and at that moment I know that in spite of everything that has happened I might just be the luckiest boy alive.

'We have news,' Lexie says when we arrive for band practice. 'We've just been offered a gig on October the first, playing at the art gallery in town. Louisa Winter is having a private view for her exhibition – and all the proceeds from the paintings sold are going to a refugee charity, the one that helped to rescue Sami!'

'Cool,' Marley says.

'It's not paid then?' Bobbi-Jo chips in. 'I thought we were only looking for paid gigs? If we do things for free, people won't value us!'

'This is different,' I say. 'She offered to pay, but this is personal! Footsteps to Freedom are an international charity . . .'

'You can't let personal feelings get in the way of logic,' Bobbi-Jo says scathingly. 'If they're an international charity, they can definitely afford to pay us. And if they can't, that old artist lady definitely can – my dad says she's probably a millionaire!'

'Bobbi-Jo, that's enough,' Marley says. 'Sami, mate, we'll definitely do the gig. No charge. OK? Louisa Winter gives us our practice space for free. No way can we charge her, and that's final!'

'Thanks, Marley.' I heave a sigh of relief. 'The press will be there – TV too – maybe. It will be something good for us, I promise!'

'I know, mate,' he says. 'We'll do it.'

Marley Hayes has a ruthless streak a mile wide, but beneath the ego he does care. He's a complicated person, with kindness and arrogance battling it out inside him. Bobbi-Jo is a different case altogether. She's determined to get her claws into Marley and hang on to his coat-tails for the rollercoaster ride to fame and fortune, and she doesn't seem to care how many enemies she makes in the process.

'We're going to work on a new song specially for it,' Lexie is saying. 'Something with a refugee theme, to help raise awareness. Will you help?'

'Of course I will!' Marley says. 'That's great news! Exactly what we need. Something sad and dramatic?'

'You'll have your song,' I promise him.

*

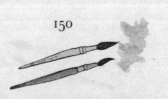

'More tea?' Ms Winter asks, pouring out a stream of a dark, woody brew that smells like bonfires into a chipped mug. 'Do you want to rest for a moment?'

In the background, a red vinyl-covered 1960s Dansette record player is crackling its way through a Kinks LP, and Ms Winter does a little dance with the mug of tea held high, before setting it down on a side table next to me.

You might not think that standing still could be so exhausting, but after almost three hours of it I can assure you that it is. I sit down on an upturned wine crate and stretch my legs, roll back my shoulders, flex my fingers. I take a cotton handkerchief from my pocket and wipe the beads of sweat from my forehead.

'Shall I open the window?' Ms Winter asks. 'Or put the fan on, perhaps? You must be baking. I do so want the overcoat in the picture, though . . .'

'I never take the overcoat off,' I tell her.

'You don't? How interesting! Why is that, Sami?'

I open my mouth to tell her that I can't talk about this, but somehow different words slip out.

'The coat was my father's,' I tell her. 'He made it, back

151

home in Damascus. It was a heavy coat to last through a hard journey, a European winter. It's all I have left of him.'

'Oh, Sami,' she whispers. 'I'm sorry.'

I shrug, reaching out to take the chipped mug of smoky tea.

'It's falling apart,' I say, picking up a frayed edge of worn-out tweed. 'Everything falls apart in the end, doesn't it?'

'Material things, yes,' Louisa Winter agrees. 'But the real treasures in this life are not material things. Memories, love, loss, courage, compassion – a lifetime of friends and family and little moments of magic, lost and found. Those things can last forever, in here . . .'

She taps the centre of her chest, bony beneath today's paint-stained denim overall.

I nod, my heart beating hard. Every person carries those secrets, I realize. Everyone has a parcel of happy and sad inside of them.

'You don't need the coat to remember your father,' Ms Winter says. 'You'll never forget him, coat or no coat. Am I right?'

'You are right,' I say, and some of the pain slides away from my shoulders, away from my heart.

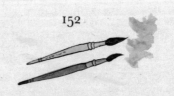

'Is the sketch working?' I ask. 'Is it good?'

We have already tried four different poses. Three abandoned drawings made with charcoal on A1 Ingres paper now litter the studio floor, with the fourth still in progress.

'Maybe,' Ms Winter says, frowning. 'Almost. But not quite. I want something strong, iconic. I want to show you striding across Europe in your tattered coat . . .'

'Playing the flute,' I say. 'With the kids running along after me, like in one of the picture books the teachers had in Thessaloniki. *The Pied Piper*, I think. Little Amira in her mud-stained princess dress and broken fairy wings, Nazz and Joe, always together, always laughing . . .'

'Did they come to Britain too?' Ms Winter asks.

I shake my head. 'Joe got ill and was taken to hospital. It was pneumonia. He . . . he didn't get better. Nazz disappeared after that. We never heard what happened to him. Amira . . . she didn't talk much, didn't eat much. She'd been separated from her family somewhere in Greece, and the sadness just ate away at her. She got sick too . . .'

I sip tea from the chipped mug, tea that takes me back to places I never wanted to think of again.

'I'm sorry,' I say. 'I never usually talk about it. Not to my social worker, not to Lexie, not to anyone.'

'I can see why,' Ms Winter says. 'But it must be very difficult to hold all that inside you. Sometimes, talking can help.'

I shake my head.

It just wasn't possible at the start to speak about the past, no matter what Ben, my social worker, said. My aunt and uncle have never pushed me to talk; they are endlessly kind and good to me, but they are quiet, reserved people with no time for counsellors or soul-baring.

'Forget the past, Sami,' Aunt Zenna once told me. 'There is too much hurt there. You have to let go, move on.'

Sometimes, though, the past creeps up on me unawares and I find my cheeks suddenly wet with tears, my heart so heavy I think it will break. I try to forget, but still I long for everything I have lost.

'Have you tried putting it down on paper? Writing it down? Drawing it?' Louisa Winter is asking me. 'That could help. Some things cannot be buried, ignored. You must face it, Sami, acknowledge it. It's a part of you. Don't let the darkness eat away at you from within.'

I nod, my throat burning with all the things I need to say and yet cannot.

Across the studio, the Dansette record player crackles to a halt, and there is silence.

I take the notebook from my pocket and hand it over to Louisa Winter, watch through a blur of tears as she reads my story.

We were about a mile from the island when it all went wrong. The wind was high and the sea was rough. A baby was crying and there was the low murmur of people praying, but already in the distance I could see the faint pink glow of daybreak and the silhouette of a low, craggy landmass that had to be Kos.

Abruptly, the outboard motor cut out. The captain yelled that it wasn't a problem, he'd have it running again in a moment, that everyone had to stay still. And we did stay still, adrift and silent on a dark, squally sea, the moonlight picking out the fear on our upturned faces as the captain tried again and again to start up the ancient engine.

For a while, the only sound was the rough drag of the starter rope, the slow buzz of the propeller fading into silence. Each time, it felt more ominous.

Suddenly, someone shouted that the boat was taking in water. I felt the slosh of cold water at my feet; fear turned my limbs to jelly. The captain was shouting again, telling everyone to stay calm, that it was just sea spray, but a kind of confused terror took hold. Men were stumbling forward, trying to find the source of the possible leak, women were trying to reach their partners, children were wriggling and screaming.

It happened so quickly: the boat, already too low in the water, was rocking from side to side like a cork on the tide. And then we listed violently to the right and the ice-cold waves of the Aegean Sea began to pour in, and the screams reached fever pitch. I hear them in my nightmares even now.

I lunged forward, grabbed my mother and my little sister and glanced behind where I was almost sure I could see my father's face, too far away in the moonlight to touch.

'I love you,' my mother whispered, soft beneath the screams all around us — and we went into the sea.

15

A Story to Tell

I go to the studio three more times in the space of a week.

The Dansette record player ploughs through ancient LPs by The Beatles, the Small Faces, the Mamas & the Papas and, of course, Ked Wilder as Louisa Winter makes endless charcoal and pastel roughs, and finally a longer study in chalk and charcoal of me playing the flute. When the preliminary drawings and paintings are done, she takes photographs with an old-fashioned Polaroid camera – endless pictures from every angle.

At first I feel vulnerable, way too visible after years of trying to hide, but after a while I learn to switch off and allow my mind to drift away. I'm back in Syria, playing football in the street, watching the stars on the roof with my dad's arm wrapped round my shoulders. I'm in the camp on the Turkish border, watching the worry lines on my mother's face etch deeper each day, seeing my little sister's eyes fill up with fear. I'm in the camp on Kos, my heart broken into a million pieces, shivering in a tent in Thessaloniki with Nazz and Joe and Amira, walking through countries I never even knew existed until I had to cross them. I'm playing the flute, walking ahead while the little kids follow, wondering still if I am keeping them safe or leading them into danger and realizing I can never know for sure.

The last time I go to the studio, the studies and Polaroids are pinned up all around us, and a huge stretched canvas waits, propped against one wall, the basic shapes already mapped out in thin sepia paint.

'I have everything I need,' Ms Winter tells me. 'Thank you, Sami. You've been a wonderful model . . . you wear your heart on your sleeve. Or, to be more accurate, your eyes give away so much of what you've been through. I just need to shut myself away to capture it in paint now. That's the difficult bit, and also the exciting bit!'

'You don't need me to model any more?' I check.

'No, no, you're free again, Sami, with my very great thanks,' she says. 'I thought we'd just have one last cup of tea, one last chat. The thing is, I have a confession to make. The other day, when you left me your notebook to read . . .'

I frown. I left the notebook with Ms Winter for a couple of hours that first day: the time it took to go to band practice. I collected it again on the way home, and it's in my pocket now.

'Yes?' I say, watching the old lady pour tea, setting the mugs on a wine crate beside one of the paint-stained sofas.

'Well, I suppose the best thing is to show you,' she says, picking up a cardboard folder. 'I was very moved by your pictures, your words. I wondered what those little ink sketches would look like outside the notebook, and I took the liberty of scanning a few.'

She hands me a small print on heavy, cream-coloured paper: an image of tents from the camp in Turkey.

'Imagine it in a small frame,' she says. 'Plain, simple, strong. Imagine your drawings and your words, stretching around one of the small rooms at the gallery, telling your story, Sami.'

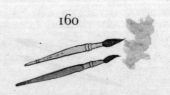

As she speaks, she hands me more sheets of paper: my mother and my sister in their life jackets; a boy walking alone along an empty beach beneath the stars; two boys grinning as they share a bowl of rice; a little girl dancing in a tattered princess dress, wearing broken fairy wings; a boy stitching ring pulls and sweet wrappers into the lining of his coat.

Outside the notebook, away from the crowded pages, the images have a power and impact that even I can see. Could they really be framed, shared? Ms Winter shows me a couple of sheets with just words, setting the pages down, alternating them with images, to show how she'd display them.

'Are you cross?' she asks me. 'I should have asked permission, I know, because these words and pictures are so very private and personal. But that's why they hold such power – that's why they matter. I hope you understand why I scanned them, but I promise I haven't shown them to another living soul, and if you're angry . . .'

'I'm not angry,' I say. 'Just surprised. Amazed.'

Ms Winter grins. 'Oh, thank goodness!' she says. 'Because I think these images tell a story that has to be told, Sami.

161

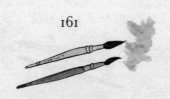

It has to be told and it has to be seen, and it would change people's minds and hearts, change the way they see refugees. The question is, are you willing to do that? To share your work, let people see?'

I frown. 'I don't understand,' I say. 'How . . .?'

Ms Winter smiles. 'My exhibition should pull in a good crowd,' she says. 'I haven't shown my work for a long time; the critics will be interested, the public too. It's a big deal for Millford's art gallery, a big deal for the charity. And if we had a small room set aside for your work – the true story of a boy who survived one of the hardest journeys of our time . . .'

I blink, still trying to make sense of it.

'My work in an art gallery?' I check.

'If you are willing to let people see,' she says.

'Is it good enough?' I ask. 'Would they want it?'

'I am certain they would want it, Sami,' she tells me. 'And yes, it's certainly good enough. When the exhibition is over and things settle down a little, you and I will have a chat about art colleges. Because that's something you should be thinking about, young man.'

I shake my head. 'I can't . . . I just don't know how. What if . . .'

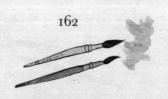

'What if I said I'd take care of it for you?' Ms Winter says. 'I'll scan the words and the pictures, clean them up, print them out, get them framed. I'll ask the gallery to set up a space for you, a side room or a small enclave within the main exhibition. I would be so very grateful, Sami. It's what the exhibition needs to give it heart and soul!'

My eyes blur, but I'm smiling as I wipe the tears away. I don't think I have a choice, not really. I have to do this, for my father, my mother, my sister, for Nazz and Joe and Amira and all the others who didn't make it. I have to do it, for all those still adrift, lost and desperate, on their own journeys.

'OK,' I say. 'I will.'

My limbs were frozen, numb, aching with exhaustion; my breath was a raw, burning ache. People hauled me out of the sea, wrapped me in blankets, held me while I vomited salt water. I was taken to a wooden hut. It had a sign that seemed to indicate you could hire bikes and surfboards there, but inside there were rows of grubby mattresses and a doctor checking that people were OK. I was given clean clothes and warm soup, and I slept the whole day, until it was almost sunset.

I have never stopped blaming myself for that. If I had woken sooner, gone out to search the beaches, perhaps I would have found them. If I had just tried a little bit harder.

Instead, I woke before sunset with a terrible fear in my soul. Where were my parents? Where was Roza? I stumbled from mattress to mattress, checking each sleeping patient. I blundered into a nearby cottage where several bedraggled travellers huddled in blankets. Some of them I recognized from the boat; some I had never seen before.

'Help me,' I pleaded with the nearest volunteer. 'I have lost my family. Our boat went down last night, and now I can't find them. My mother and sister had life jackets, but my father didn't . . .'

I spoke in Kurdish, then in Arabic, then I tried a few words of English, and used a stick to draw a boat in the sand, figures in the sea. The volunteer led me back to the hospital hut, but I shook my head, and finally she led me to a second hut, some distance from the sea, where the people laid out under bright, soft blankets were not sleeping at all but gone from this world, their faces grey, cold, so very, very still. I walked along the rows of men, women, children — but I did not find my family.

I sat down on the shoreline and put my head in my hands, and after a while a fellow Syrian came to tell me that the next high tide was coming, that there might be more bodies then.

16

Letting Go

The past is like a genie I've kept trapped inside a jar for so long that I don't quite know how to take the lid off. With or without my help, though, the genie is breaking free – it just takes one last turn of the lid to let it go.

Lexie and I are in the park with Mary Shelley, a piece of string tied round her middle so she can't stray too far. I'm lying on the grass, looking at the sky and keeping tortoise watch; Lexie is scribbling in a notebook.

'I had an idea for the song,' she says. 'But I'm worried it might be a bit too much. It's about what happened on the boat. It's going to be subtle; it doesn't spell out what's happening – but maybe it's too close to the bone?'

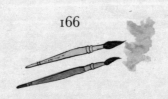

'It needs to be that way,' I tell her. 'It's OK.'

Lexie goes back to her scribbling. 'How did it feel?' she asks me after a while. 'When you went into the water?'

'I thought I would die,' I tell her. 'Everyone was screaming, my mother and my sister were trying to hold on to me, but it was impossible. I had no choice but to let the waves take me. So many people died that night, Lexie. I don't understand why I lived!'

'I'm glad you did,' she says.

'I'm glad too,' I tell her, and for the first time I actually mean it.

Mary Shelley the tortoise stops grazing and marches up to me, nudges my palm with her head. If she were a dog or a cat, I'd say she could sense how I am feeling and is offering comfort, solidarity. As it is, she's a tortoise, so . . . well, I guess it's exactly the same.

I stroke her shell gently and wonder why it is that some creatures come into this world equipped with a hard shell that protects them from danger, while others have nothing but soft skin and flesh – no armour at all. Human beings have to make their own armour, their own shell, and it might keep predators at bay, but it also stops people from

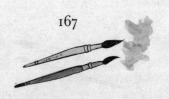

getting too close. I always thought that was a fair trade-off, but now I'm not so sure.

I roll on to one side and trail a finger over the little tortoise's head. Do tortoises wonder what life without a shell might be like? Probably not.

Back at my uncle and aunt's house, I close the bedroom door and step in front of the long wall mirror. I see a boy with bird's-nest hair and burning grey eyes that hold a world of pain. I see a boy in an ancient overcoat, a ridiculous overcoat – too big, too hot, too heavy. I see a boy in a threadbare suit of armour, a shell to protect him from the world, a shell that's worn out and no longer needed.

I peel off the overcoat, drop it on to the bed – a whole heap of love and grief and memories. I feel lighter without it, as if I've shed a skin. I haven't worked out yet whether I can function without that skin, but I'll figure it out. It's time to let go.

Aunt Zenna would probably pick up the coat between her thumb and forefinger and take it out to the wheelie bins behind the shop; she'd drop it in with all the rubbish, slam the lid shut. She'd say 'good riddance'.

I can't do that.

I love this coat. I still have all the things I found in its pockets: the hard plastic box with my father's passport and photographs inside, his mobile phone. There'd been money too, two hundred euros in small notes that I used along the way when things were desperate.

The things are in a shoebox underneath my bed, and I take them out now, spread them across the duvet cover. My father's treasures, kept safe from the Aegean Sea.

I pick up the phone, press the button, but it's dead, like my long gone father. I'd give anything to speak to my father one last time, tell him how the coat kept me warm and safe all the way across Europe, how the love he'd stitched into every seam had wrapped itself around me and pulled me back from a hundred different dangers and bad decisions. I'd tell my father that I love him, that I'm doing OK, that I finally made it to Britain and to safety.

I know he wouldn't be able to hear that voicemail – but somehow, on some level, he'd get the message and understand.

I think of Lexie, leaving letters and notes for her missing mother, and my heart aches. She told me to find a charger,

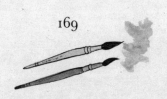

leave a message for real – is that such a crazy idea? The internet can supply just about anything these days. I pick up my own phone and search eBay, find the right charger for less than a quid and click to order it. If I can get the mobile to work, leave a message, it could be my way of saying goodbye.

I find a hanger, slide the old overcoat on to it and place it carefully on the hook on my bedroom door. Inside I can see the tattered lining, the glint of silver stuff I stitched into it on the journey, desperate to keep that lining silver even as the fabric frayed and the colour faded. Ring pulls, silver paper, a lost earring, a piece of foil tray . . . not so long ago, they'd seemed like treasure, magic. Now they just look like what they are: random bits of rubbish sewn into a tatty old coat.

Is it possible to revive the magic?

I look at the coat for a long time, then I scrabble around for a half-filled school sketchbook, pick up a pen and start to draw.

I found my father's body a mile or so from the bay, washed up on a small sandy beach in the moonlight. I knew it was him straight away, because he was still wearing the tweed coat with the silver lining — I'd have known that anywhere, but my father himself was harder to recognize. The cold water had turned his skin a terrible grey; his lips were blue-black. Salt crusted his wavy dark hair and clung like glitter to his brows, his jaw, his cheekbones.

My father would never make it to London now, and my mother and sister were still lost, perhaps lost forever at the bottom of the sea. I wanted to yell and scream and roar my pain, but in the end I just laid my head on my father's chest and cried, listening for the beat of a heart that would never come again.

When I had no more tears, I gently tugged the tweed overcoat from my father's body. It took much longer than you'd think. I wanted something to remember him by, and the big overcoat with the silver lining was something he had made himself; it was far warmer than the jacket I'd lost in the sea. I carried it up beyond the beach and hung it on an olive tree to dry, and then I sat with my father's body until distant searchlights signalled the arrival of the volunteers.

17

Song for the Sea

The first time I leave the flat without the ancient overcoat, Aunt Zenna goes crazy. 'At last, at last!' she shrieks, pulling me back into the hallway. 'I knew you would see sense! I knew you would listen, in the end! At last we can get rid of that horrible old rag!'

'I am keeping the coat,' I tell her firmly. 'It's all I have left of my father!'

Aunt Zenna nods. 'I know,' she tells me. 'I understand, Sami. We can put it away then, keep it safe. When you're ready. But look at you, so clean and handsome and well-dressed! I'm just so happy to see you without it, looking like a normal boy!'

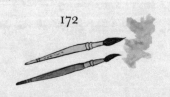

I'm looking as normal as I ever have, I suppose, in Converse and skinny jeans and a white T-shirt with a blue plaid shirt layered over the top – after years of hiding in the overcoat, I feel underdressed without it. It doesn't matter how I look, though. I'm not like everyone else; I never can be.

'I am so proud of you,' Aunt Zenna declares, and pulls me in for a quick hug before running a critical hand through my hair. 'Next, we'll book you a haircut! You look like you've been sleeping in a hedge!'

'Don't push your luck,' I tell her, and drop a quick kiss on her cheek before heading down the stairs.

On the street I feel conspicuous, as if everyone is looking at me, laughing at me; in fact, I know that now they no longer have reason to stare or laugh. People often made comments about the overcoat: kids laughed at it, teachers huffed, old ladies tutted and shook their heads. The coat was frayed and stained and scruffy, but it was part of me. Without it, I feel exposed, raw, vulnerable.

I meet Lexie at the park, watch her do a double take as she sees me.

'No coat?' she checks, as if I have it hidden somewhere. 'Really? That's awesome! How does it feel?'

'Weird,' I tell her. 'Scary. Disloyal. But also like I'm breaking free, moving forward. It's hard to explain!'

'You're explaining it well,' she says, and I am glad that Lexie has read my notebooks and knows the story behind the overcoat, knows why I wore it, loved it, hid beneath it.

'What will you do with it?' she wants to know. 'The coat. Store it away somehow?'

'Maybe,' I tell her. 'Eventually. But for now, I have some ideas for it. I want to repair it, patch it up, add a bit more to the lining perhaps . . .'

I open my palm to reveal a silver bottle top, a shard of glass, a twist of shiny silver wire. 'I think it's going to be a kind of art project; keep a lookout for silver stuff. And feathers!'

'OK. Sounds mysterious, but I will,' Lexie says. 'I'll actually miss that coat, y'know. Even before I got to know you properly, you were the boy with the big overcoat and the cool hair. You stood out from the crowd. And now you have to learn to live without it, learn to blend in. No more magic coat.'

'Blame Mary Shelley,' I say. 'She got me thinking about the advantages and disadvantages of having a hard shell. I decided to do without. I'm done with hiding.'

'Well, I liked the coat, but I'm glad you don't need it any more,' she says. She puts an arm around me. I feel the warmth of her skin burning into my body, and I'm glad too.

Later, at the old railway carriage, I get a whole load more positive comments and even a hug from Marley.

'Mate,' he says. 'You look amazing! I hated that old rag of a coat, y'know!'

'I know you did,' I say.

'It was a health hazard,' Bobbi-Jo says. 'An eyesore. Yuck!'

But the rest of the band understand how much the coat means to me, even though they don't know why, and their comments are kind and low-key. I am the topic of the day for all of five minutes, and then Marley shuts down the chat by announcing that he's put in our entry for the Battle of the Bands.

'We're in the studio with Barney Bright two weeks on Friday,' he explains. 'It's the last slot in the competition, because he says he knows all about us and wants to save the best till last. Good, huh?'

Bobbi-Jo shrugs. 'I asked him to,' she says. 'The last band to play is the one the voters will remember – hopefully!

And of course he knows all about you – I tell him all the time!'

'We need to decide what we're going to play,' Marley points out. 'Sami and Lexie have come up with some new lyrics, and we're working on a melody for them now, so we should have something for everyone to work on soon.'

'Hope it's upbeat,' she says.

'An upbeat song about the refugee crisis?' Marley says. 'I don't think so! We're going for powerful and emotional. The question is, will it be the best choice for the competition? I guess we can see how it turns out and make a final call later this week.'

Bobbi-Jo pulls a face. 'Dad says there are quite a few entries already,' she tells us. 'He's going to start airing the entrants one a day, starting on Monday, and there's lots of hype about getting people to vote. It should be good! I know that Pretty Street have put their name down. T-Dawg is still nagging me to join them as a dancer. He's very persistent . . .'

'Not tempted?' Bex asks, looking hopeful.

'Not really,' Bobbi-Jo says with a shrug. 'I don't want to waste my time with amateur outfits. I think we're going to make it, and I'll get Dad to manage us, get us signed by

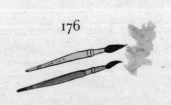

one of the big labels. I mean, I wouldn't be here otherwise!
I want a career in the music business. I'm determined!'

'More's the pity,' Bex says under her breath.

Luckily, Bobbi-Jo doesn't hear.

Song for the Sea

Crashing arms summon me,
As the wind cries overhead
I look into your eyes
Taste those salty lips
I hold out my hand
And lean my back into the wind.
Will you catch me if I fall?
Will you have me at all?
At all . . .

I dip below the waves
Holding my everlasting breath
Bodies float in the moonlight
While my mind drifts away
One day I'll come to you and stay . . .
Will you catch me if I fall?
Will you have me here at all?
At all.

I've never been part of the songwriting process before, but this time Lexie and Marley make sure I'm involved in every step. It's fascinating to see how the two of them bounce ideas off each other. Marley takes the words Lexie writes and plays around with sound and melody, working up a couple of possible approaches. Lexie and I are instinctively drawn to one of them, and then it's a case of perfecting the tune and adjusting the chorus to fit with this.

The overall sound is simple, spare, melancholic . . . but with powerful sweeps of violin and flute that sneak their way into your soul and won't let go. Marley works up a basic three-note rhythm for Bobbi-Jo to play, something so simple that even she won't be able to go wrong. He asks Jake to find a sound sample of waves breaking on the shore to use as an intro and fade out for the song.

The first time we play it as a band, my heart aches so hard I think it might break . . . Sasha's voice is so pure, so haunting. She's been quiet and daydreamy these last few weeks, as if there's something on her mind, but the moment she has the new song lyrics she's back on form – and how.

It takes a while for the rest of us to pull it all together – Lee

has an idea for a dramatic trumpet solo in the middle, George comes up with an amazing cello piece to ease the transition from the waves sample to the music – but finally the new song is sounding tight.

'It might even be the best thing we've done,' Marley declares. 'Sasha's totally nailed those vocals and the harmonies are heartbreakingly good. Sami's flute solo gives me the shivers. This is special – I think we're on to a winner!'

The Battle of the Bands competitors begin airing every afternoon on *The Barney Bright Show*, and we tune in daily to hear our rivals. School bully Sharleen starts things off with a screechy version of a Katy Perry song; Jake's stepdad's ceilidh band plays an eightsome reel, and there are lacklustre performances from assorted other contenders we have never heard of. That first week, nobody scores more than a hundred votes.

The second week, we listen to Zombie Massacre, then the middle-aged ska band and a small girl singing 'Silent Night' – all poll almost two hundred votes, although we're pretty sure that Rick from Zombie Massacre has rigged the voting somehow, or maybe just got his mother to ring in repeatedly. On Thursday, the one and only Pretty Street have their slot. The schoolboy rap band are actually not bad, if you like that kind of thing – their entry, 'Pretty Street Sweet', is a clever rap about falling for a beautiful girl who just doesn't want to know.

'Inspired by anyone we know?' Bex asks, and Bobbi-Jo smirks.

Their performance gets an impressive 323 votes.

'We can beat them,' Marley promises. 'Easy. Remember to get your families and friends to vote. We'll meet at midday tomorrow for a final run-through, and then head to the radio station. Good luck, people!'

And, just like that, our slot for Battle of the Bands rolls around.

I stayed on Kos for two months, waiting for news of my mother and sister, but no news came. They were not on the island, nor were there any reports of them on mainland Greece. The volunteers on Kos gave me a new rucksack, new boots, new clothes, a proper bunk bed in a converted shack to sleep in. When it was clear that the rest of my family were not going to appear, they bought me a ticket for the ferry and sent me with a lot of other refugees to the mainland.

I lived that first winter in Thessaloniki, in a little tented village. Charity workers handed out jumpers and hats and gloves and thick woollen socks, but if you have ever tried living in a tent in January you will know it is not much fun. It was impossible to keep anything clean, impossible to get properly warm. I wasn't the only lone kid there; there were gangs of us, running half feral without our families, wild with grief and the sudden freedom. We stuck together, sharing tents on the edge of the camp close to where the charity workers stayed, and they kept an eye on us, made sure we had food, dry bedding, books, medicine.

I shared a tent with two younger boys, Nazz and Joe, and a girl called Amira who can't have been more than five. Nazz was from Iraq, Joe from Syria like me and Amira wouldn't talk about her family or her home, but she spoke Arabic and she stuck to us like glue. I came to see her as a sort of little sister. We were all heading for Britain, and we looked out for each other, shared food and blankets, sat up late at night, burning litter and foraged brushwood in a tin-can bonfire and drinking stewed black tea with sugar from battered enamel mugs.

'When I get to England, I'm going to be a famous footballer,' Nazz declared. 'Ronaldo, Wayne Rooney, David Beckham! And me!'

'Me too,' Joe said. 'Or maybe a film star! Hollywood!'

'Hollywood's not in England,' I told him, but he wouldn't believe me.

Amira didn't say much, but she never walked if she could dance, and sometimes when I was playing the flute beside the bonfire, she'd sing, her little voice clear and strong. The other kids would come over then, and we'd share songs from Syria and Afghanistan and Iraq, songs from all the places that had pushed us out of our homes and into the big, bad world. Sometimes we played football with bundles of rags tied together with string, and sometimes there would be a real football, or an empty crate to turn into a go-cart with broken pram wheels and bits of string.

Not everybody was kind. Men from outside the camp would offer us kids hundreds of euros to join some scheme or other: picking fruit in Italy, going to a refugee school in Germany, working at a beach resort in Bulgaria. We would have instant citizenship, they promised, but the older kids told us not to listen to them, that there would be no fruit picking, no school, no beach; it was just some dodgy scam that would end badly.

Every night Nazz would zigzag string hung with empty tin cans across the tent doorway, an elaborate trap to wake us if anyone tried to get in.

'This'll keep us safe,' he used to say, and it still grieves me that I couldn't keep Nazz safe, that I was the only one of the four of us to make it to Britain.

18

Star of the Show

'There's nothing to be scared of,' Bobbi-Jo tells us as we wait to be called into the studio at Millford Sounds Radio. 'I've been here millions of times.'

'To play?' Lee asks, and Bobbi-Jo gives him a scathing look.

'Obviously not. Look, I was thinking – "Song for the Sea" is sounding good, but it needs something more intricate from the keyboards. I've been working on something . . .'

'No,' Marley says firmly. 'We've got everything perfect. We only get one shot at this – let's not start meddling now. We play what we've practised, OK?'

Bobbi-Jo scowls, but she doesn't argue.

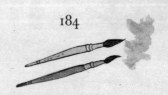

An assistant arrives to take us to a side studio, and we take the drum kit through and set up everything else around it. A couple of sound guys mooch around checking that everything's where it should be, and then we do a soundcheck so they can get the levels right. After a couple of false starts, everyone is happy with the levels and Sasha is belting out the lyrics with passion. The rest of us are pitch perfect – except Bobbi-Jo. In spite of Marley's warning, she is playing a completely different tune, making her piece a jumble of dud notes and tinny melody.

'What do we do?' Lexie asks Marley once the sound guys disappear and Bobbi-Jo is at a safe distance, listening to *The Barney Bright Show* through a fancy headphone set. 'She's going to wreck our chances. She just can't follow instructions, and she has no idea how bad she is . . .'

'I know,' Marley agrees. 'I have a fall-back plan. I'm going to unplug her sound lead. It's the only way!'

'Unplug her?' Lexie whispers, aghast. 'So nobody actually hears her? She'll go nuts!'

'Only if she finds out.' Marley shrugs. 'Look, we don't have a choice! Trust me. It'll be fine!'

Bobbi-Jo turns back to us, grinning, sliding the headphones

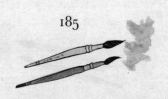

from her ears. 'Dad's just announced that we'll be on right after the three o'clock news, so he should be through any minute!'

'Cool,' Marley says to Bobbi-Jo. 'Just focus and stick to the piece you've been practising. No fancy extra bits; it's just going to confuse matters, OK? Can I trust you on that?'

'Of course!' Bobbi-Jo says grudgingly.

'Also, when we're all amplified, it can sound a bit different from normal,' Marley explains. 'You can't always get the whole picture; you have to trust that the sound guys have got it mixed perfectly. They will have. Just don't panic if it sounds like you're not making any sound – that sometimes happens!'

'It does?' Bobbi-Jo questions. 'How weird!'

'Yeah, weird,' Marley agrees. 'But the listeners will be able to hear, so just keep doing your thing and everything will be fine!'

The rest of us exchange glances, trying not to look guilty about colluding to keep Bobbi-Jo's contribution to the song strictly unplugged, and I almost miss the moment when Marley casually swipes the lead from the keyboard. The deed is done.

Barney Bright comes in then, grinning broadly and shaking everyone by the hand. 'I've heard a lot about you,' he says. 'Bobbi-Jo never stops talking about you! I hear she's quite the star of the show!'

'Er – that's right,' Marley says, his face frozen, awkward. 'Something like that. We're very glad to have her on board!'

'Well, rather you than me,' the DJ barges on. 'It's taken thirteen years for someone to unearth Bobbi-Jo's musical talent. Always thought she was tone deaf, myself; the only one in the family who skipped the musical talent gene! Maybe she'll prove me wrong after all!'

I glance at Lexie, wide-eyed. We're all slightly shocked at Barney Bright's harsh words, and I notice that Bobbi-Jo is staring at her shoes, a flush of crimson staining her cheeks. Her pushy ways are clearly a family trait, but underneath them is a little kid trying desperately hard to win some praise. I can't help feeling sorry for her. On the outside, she looks like the luckiest girl in the world, but maybe inside she's as lost as the rest of us.

'So the news will be on for, what, another four minutes,' Barney Bright is saying. 'As soon as it finishes, I'll introduce

187

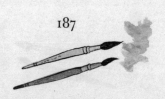

you. I'll ask you, Marley, to say a few words about why you think people should vote for you. Sound OK?'

'Perfect,' Marley says.

'And then you'll go straight into your piece – "Song for the Sea", yes? Remember it's live, so give it all you've got!'

'No pressure then,' Marley jokes, but some of the band are looking distinctly uncomfortable. Romy looks like she'd bolt out of the door given half a chance, and Sasha is fanning herself with a printout of the lyrics.

Barney Bright pulls his headphones back on and hands a spare set to Marley, and we watch the clock tick round agonizingly slowly. Suddenly, Barney launches into a high-energy intro about the Battle of the Bands.

'Some might say we've saved the best till last,' he crows. 'But I'd better let you be the judge of that! The Lost & Found are young, talented and tipped for the top – by none other than sixties pop legend Ked Wilder! They wowed audiences at Millford's recent Protest Festival in support of the libraries, but can they wow listeners today? Marley Hayes, lead guitarist and brains behind the band, what do *you* think?'

'I think Ked Wilder might be on to something,' Marley

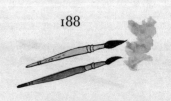

quips, confident as ever. 'I'm not about to argue with him, anyway! We are young – we all go to Millford Park Academy, or most of us, anyway – and we're quite a big band, twelve of us in all. We like to think we're a little bit different; our music has heart and soul.

'We'd be thrilled to win the Battle of the Bands because we are passionate about what we do and we want to get to the very top! We're going to play you our newest song, based on the experiences of one of our band members who is a Syrian refugee. I'm warning you, it's a tear-jerker, so keep those tissues handy!'

I grit my teeth and look daggers at Marley, but he's too hyped to notice.

'Ladies and gentlemen, this is "Song for the Sea"!'

There's a moment of silence, and then into the silence comes the sound of waves breaking on the shoreline, timed perfectly by Jake. As the sample fades away, George begins his cello piece and I step forward, my flute solo piercing the air and setting the scene for Sasha to step up to the mic and sing.

Except that she doesn't. The guitar, bass, drums and keyboards all come in on time, but Sasha stands frozen,

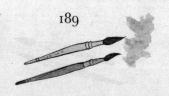

silent, her face blank, staring. A trickle of perspiration runs down from her forehead, but she doesn't seem to notice. Is it stage fright? Panic? Is she ill?

I reach out, touch her elbow.

'You OK?' I ask, and Sasha looks up at me, frowning, as if she can't quite work out what's happening.

'You missed your cue!' Marley hisses under his breath as the various instruments crash to an undignified halt. 'Get a grip, Sasha! This is no time to flake out on us!'

'Sorry!' Sasha's cheeks flood with colour and she wipes the sweat from her brow as Lexie offers her cold water, kind words.

'Sorry, folks, a small technical hitch there,' Barney Bright is saying. 'The joys of live radio, hey? Never work with children and animals! Hahaha! Let's take that from the beginning!'

Quietly, the sound guy steps up out of nowhere to reconnect Bobbi-Jo's keyboard. The bloke is clearly too good; even in that twenty seconds of chaos, he noticed it was unplugged and jumped in to sort it. Our fate is sealed.

'From the top!' Marley shouts, and Jake's sampled intro begins again. This time, Sasha, still looking shaken, takes

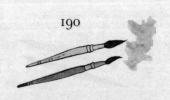

her cue at exactly the right moment and starts to sing. Her voice is heartbreakingly clear. Also heartbreakingly clear are Bobbi-Jo's keyboard skills, or, rather, the lack of them. Dud notes and a mortifying switch to synth style in the last section seem to drown out the perfect harmonies, the violin and cello pieces, the little trumpet solo. It's all I can hear: a jangle of discord.

'Well, I think we can all agree that after a slightly sticky start, that was really, um, interesting,' Barney Bright booms. 'Listeners, if you want to vote for the Lost & Found, pick up your phones now and make a call.'

He goes on to list the cost of calling from a landline as opposed to a mobile, and explains that the lines will be open until six o'clock before lining up a new R&B track and sliding off his headset.

'Bit of a dog's dinner, that,' he says bluntly, the minute we're off air. 'That's the trouble with teen bands. Inconsistent. All talk and no talent – and as usual, I let myself fall for it. By the way, I'd get yourselves a new keyboardist, if I were you . . .'

He heads back to the main studio, leaving us to dismantle the drum kit and pack up. We trudge across town in silence.

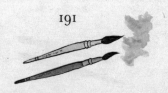

Back at the old railway carriage, we dump our stuff and Sasha bows her head and starts to sob.

'It wasn't your fault,' Lexie tells her, although Marley's stony face suggests that he thinks it was. 'Stage fright can happen to anyone. You sang beautifully!'

'What did Dad mean about getting a new keyboardist?' Bobbi-Jo asks, clearly confused. 'It was Sasha who missed her cue! Did I mess up too? I didn't mean to. I was just trying to make the keyboard part more interesting. Was it my fault?'

'Not really,' Bex says with a sigh. 'It just wasn't our day.'

'Maybe it's the keyboard,' Bobbi-Jo ploughs on. 'Let's face it – this one's not the best, is it?'

Marley rolls his eyes, exasperated. 'Whatever,' he says. 'Anyhow, I don't think your dad wants to be our manager – he made that clear.'

I think the rest of us are quite relieved about that. Barney Bright is too brash, too sharp-tongued by far, whatever his musical connections. I remember how he spoke to his daughter, how crushed and embarrassed Bobbi-Jo looked. I am pretty sure that all she wants from life is a single word of praise or respect from her father, and also pretty sure she'll never get it.

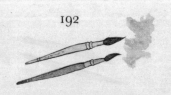

'Look, I'll make it up to you,' Bobbi-Jo is pleading. 'I promise! I'll do whatever it takes! Besides, the votes aren't in yet . . . we could still win!'

I think she is the only one to actually believe that. When the votes are counted, it turns out we've polled 312 to come in just behind Pretty Street, and it's a miracle we managed that. Marley looks sick with shame.

'I really thought we had something,' Lexie says to me that evening as we sit together on the rusty old fire escape behind the dry-cleaning shop. 'I thought that song was powerful, that it could win. I'm gutted, Sami!'

'The song is good,' I tell her. 'We just didn't play well on the day.'

Lexie has a kid's jar of bubble mixture, bought from the newsagent on the corner; she's showing me how to use the little wand to blow skeins of bubbles across the warm evening air. They drift out beyond the half-filled skip from the charity shop next door, iridescent, magical. They make me think of Nazz and Joe and Amira, and how much they'd have loved this spectacle.

'Sasha feels awful,' Lexie frowns. 'It's not like her to mess

up like that, and I even felt sorry for Bobbi-Jo. No wonder she's so pushy – her dad's horrible, and she's desperate for a bit of praise from him!'

'Not someone we want for a manager,' I agree. 'I think we had a lucky escape.'

Lexie blows a bubble at my face, and it pops as it touches my cheek; one moment it's a perfect sphere of shiny possibility, the next it's a smear of diluted soap, drying to nothing. If we're not careful, the Lost & Found could find that their bubble bursts too.

'Marley's going to have a mutiny on his hands if he doesn't sort things out,' I say.

Lexie puts down the bubble mixture and snuggles closer, dropping her head on to my shoulder.

'Yeah, Marley's lost the plot this summer,' she agrees. 'He was convinced we'd win; all his plans hinged on that.'

But we've lost, and Marley's hopes and dreams are done for.

By spring, we were on the move again. We travelled to the Macedonian border, a long line of us, carrying our belongings on our backs. Some families pushed wheelbarrows filled with tents and toddlers, some pushed grandparents in wheelchairs, some walked quickly and some sat down at the roadside and peeled off socks and boots to reveal feet that were raw with blisters and sores.

We walked along roads and railway tracks, through fields and villages. We walked right through Macedonia and into Serbia, and then on and on through Serbia and into Hungary. Sometimes when we passed through towns and villages we were given sandwiches and fruit and chocolate. Sometimes we were yelled at, spat on, screamed at. In some places, soldiers stopped us camping.

'Why do they hate us so?' Amira would ask, but I had no answer. I didn't know.

When Nazz and Joe and Amira got tired, I played my flute, even though the sound was less than perfect now. The kids gathered close and we walked together, like an illustration from the story of the Pied Piper in the picture book I'd read with them in Thessaloniki. We'd started out as a group of four, but as we trekked through Eastern Europe more kids tagged on until there were maybe fifteen of us. I was the kid with the big coat and the flute, the kid the little ones followed.

I'd started collecting silver stuff by then, bright rubbish found by the side of the road: tiny bits of scrap metal, silver wire, foil. At night I would sit by the bonfire and stitch those things into the lining of my coat.

'Magic,' Amira said.

Sometimes when we stopped to rest, to eat an apple or some bread or cheese, I would spread the coat wide around me so that the littlest ones could snuggle in. Sometimes when I spread my arms wide and lifted up the front panels of the coat, it looked as though I had wings.

19

A Work of Art

Once upon a time, not so long ago, my life was set out before me like the pattern pieces of a suit, cut from good fabric and ready to sew. I knew what it would look like, and I knew it would be a perfect fit.

Now, those pattern pieces are torn and spoiled, like the worn-out silver lining of my father's old overcoat. I can't see how to stitch anything at all from them, but still, I am determined to try.

I train myself once more to look for silver things – foil wrappings, squashed aluminium cans, paper clips, tinsel. I collect feathers too – soft white feathers, mottled grey ones, tiny downy ones. I take some time every day to stitch my treasures into the coat.

'Oh, Sami, it's worse than ever!' my aunt laments.

But I think it's a work of art.

Bobbi-Jo doesn't appear for Monday's practice and, after waiting ten minutes for her, Marley decrees that we get started anyway. 'We'll run through the covers,' he says fiercely. 'We can't let this setback get to us. Let's give it all we've got!'

After two or three songs, we begin to relax and enjoy the rehearsal – and it sounds good too, perhaps because there are no keyboard disasters.

We're halfway through 'Dancing in the Street', the mood lighter than it's been for weeks, when Bobbi-Jo bounds into the railway carriage and starts waving her arms around.

'Listen!' she screeches above the sound of our playing. 'Big news! Stop playing, quick – Mum's waiting for me in the car!'

The song limps to a premature finish, and Bobbi-Jo looks around, beaming.

'OK,' she announces. 'Wait till you hear this! I need all of you to clear your diaries for tomorrow – no excuses, no arguments! You will not believe this!'

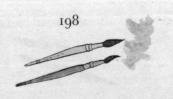

'Believe what?' Jake wants to know. 'What's going on?'

'We're in the studio,' she declares. 'All day! I got my dad to call his friend, the one with the recording studio. They've had a last-minute cancellation, and we can take it, free of charge.'

I frown. 'But we lost!' I say. 'We didn't win the studio time, so how come . . .?'

'Don't ask,' Bobbi-Jo says. 'I begged my dad, all right? I got my mum to argue for me. I said we'd had a bad day and reminded him how close that result was – there were just eleven votes in it. I told them that we picked the wrong song, that we'd record something better on the day. He pulled some strings. It's short notice, I know, but we all need to be at the studio tomorrow bright and early!'

Marley blinks. 'You've got us studio time?' he checks. 'No way! That's amazing, Bobbi-Jo!'

'I knew you'd be pleased!' she says. 'I pulled out all the stops to get this opportunity for us. This is our big break!'

Silence settles over the railway carriage, awkward and uneasy.

'Are we actually ready for this?' Dylan asks. 'With things the way they are just now? What about Ked Wilder? Shouldn't we wait to see what he thinks?'

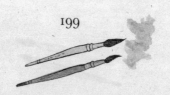

'For goodness' sake,' Bobbi-Jo snaps. 'We can't sit around forever waiting for that old fossil to remember we exist – we have to take control! Marley and me have a clear vision for the band. We have to move forward, and if anyone's not up to scratch, they're out!'

She shoots a dark look at Sasha, who wilts visibly under her glare.

'I feel awful about Friday,' Sasha says. 'I don't know what happened. One minute I was stressing about getting everything right, the next minute I'd blown it and everyone was staring at me. I don't understand it. I'm really, really sorry!'

'We all have our off days, Sasha,' Lee says. 'It could have been any of us.'

'We just weren't good enough on the day,' Jake agrees.

The others chip in their support, and Happi, Romy, Bex and Lexie step forward to give Sasha a group hug.

'Forget about Friday,' Marley cuts in. 'This is a fresh start – let's make the most of it. We need a single. Our stuff needs to be up on SoundCloud and Bandcamp and Spotify. We need reviews and publicity – not just in the local paper but nationally. We've had a setback – let's put it behind us, move on!'

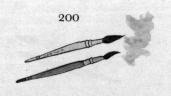

'What's all this about you two having a clear vision for the band?' Bex asks. 'Where does that leave the rest of us?'

'Someone's got to think big,' Bobbi-Jo says with a shrug. 'And sometimes you have to make quick decisions, right? If we hadn't taken this cancellation, there might not have been another chance for ages!'

'We're still a team,' Marley says. 'We always will be – but Bobbi-Jo's right, not everything can be decided by group vote!'

'Not anything, lately,' Bex grumbles.

'We need to pick a song for the single,' Marley pushes on. 'I think we should go for "Train of Thought", because "Song for the Sea" just didn't work for us on Friday. If anyone disagrees, just say. Everyone's views count. Teamwork, right?'

I stare at Marley, dismayed – using 'Song for the Sea' as our first single would have been the perfect way to get the refugee message out there, but he isn't even considering the idea. He can't meet my eye. Nobody argues, but Lexie shakes her head and reaches out to squeeze my hand.

'Just be there tomorrow,' Bobbi-Jo snaps. 'If you lot get the eight-twenty train from Millford, I'll get on at Brookleigh.

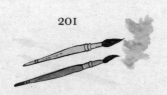

Don't let me down, OK? I really had to sweet-talk my dad to swing this!'

Lexie is the first to break the silence. 'OK,' she says. 'Thanks. We'll be there. We won't let you down.'

'Good,' she says. 'Look . . . I'm skipping practice today. Like I said, Mum drove me over; I can't keep her waiting much longer. Get yourselves sorted – I'll take the keyboard and meet you on the train in the morning.'

She blows a kiss in Marley's direction and walks away across the grass, keyboard case swinging.

'She gets the wrong end of the stick sometimes,' Marley says into the stony silence.

'Mainly because you won't tell her the truth,' Bex snarls. 'I'm not that girl's greatest fan, but anyone can tell she's sweet on you. She must be majorly short-sighted, but that's not the point. Come clean – tell her you're gay. It's no biggie!'

'I will, eventually,' he says with a sigh. 'Just not yet . . .'

I can see things crumbling, falling to pieces right in front of me. We're just a bunch of kids in an old railway carriage, playing a lot of mismatched instruments and singing songs that a few weeks ago had the power to send shivers down

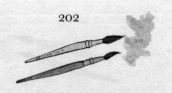

my spine, the power to make a festival crowd of several thousand people scream themselves hoarse in the hope of an encore. We had something special. Ked Wilder knew it, the TV people knew it, the newspapers knew it – but things have changed since then.

These days, our music is more likely to curdle milk than send shivers down anyone's spine. Everyone but Marley knows it, and right now we have a revolution on our hands.

'Bobbi-Jo knows what she's doing,' Marley argues. 'She's not stupid – she knows her keyboard skills aren't great. She's bluffing her way through because she wants to be famous. If I am using her – and I don't think I am – she's using me just as much. She wants her dad's approval, and this might just do it. He might still agree to manage us if this works out!'

'Do we want him as our manager?' Bex asks. 'I looked him up on the internet last night. That boy band he managed, the Bright Boys, broke up after a couple of hits; they sued him for mismanagement. He ripped them off, basically – they never made a penny!'

Marley looks as though he might cry. 'OK, we don't have to have him as a manager. Just let's give this a go!'

Bex shakes her head. 'If we record a dud single, it won't

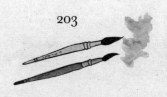

make the band – it'll break it! You need a reality check, Marley. Besides, this thing isn't just about fame!'

'I know,' he says. 'I've got this, I promise. I'll suggest to the mixing guy that Bobbi-Jo records her track after we lay down the guitar, bass and vocals. Maybe some of it will be usable, but whatever happens, I'll get Bobbi-Jo out of there by midday. We'll have the option of a back-up plan. I do share your concerns and I know a lot of you aren't sure about Bobbi-Jo . . .'

'We're sure all right,' Dylan mutters. 'Sure she's hopeless!'

'The plan is that Sasha also records the keyboard piece,' Marley goes on. 'If it's better – let's face it, it will be – we'll ask the sound guys to use that. Bobbi-Jo need never know that it's not her playing on the single.'

It's a sly move, a sneaky move, and I can tell with one glance that Lexie feels just as uncomfortable with the deception as I do, but the relief of our band mates is clear. Lee blows a trumpet salute and Bex chucks a cushion from one of the bench seats at Marley's head, which he dodges, laughing.

The revolution has been averted, and we have peace again – for now.

The coat was my protection against the cold and the rain, my shelter, my blanket on warm nights along the way. It was the only link I had to my father, but after a soaking in the Aegean, a winter in Thessaloniki and months on the road, it was starting to fray. The glossy grey satin lining was thin and torn in places, losing its shine.

It began slowly, the silver-lining stuff. I'd find an old Coke can by the side of the road and snip it open, flatten out the tin and cut it into little star shapes, then stitch them into the lining. I started collecting ring pulls, silver foil, scraps of grey and silver fabric and, once, a muddied silver sequinned scarf. Sometimes I'd find a silver ribbon, a broken bracelet, a sweet wrapper, a twist of wire. The kids would find things and bring them to me, and in the evenings I would stitch a crazy patchwork of silver into the coat.

My father's carefully stitched silver lining was falling apart, but I was doing everything I could to keep it shining. It was a way of keeping hope alive, of hanging on to the memories of my father.

I had stopped believing in silver linings a year before, on the beach in Kos, but the truth was that every single one of the kids I was travelling with had a story just as sad, just as shocking as mine. We were lost, alone, every one of us, and those little kids . . . they needed something to believe in.

20

A Crowded Train

If you have ever tried to travel on a rush-hour train in almost tropical heat with nine friends and a full-size drum kit, you will know that it's not much fun.

Jake has slept in and texts to say he'll follow in an hour, but he's our tech guy rather than a main player so Marley shrugs and manages not to freak out. George has his cello and Marley and Bex have bulky guitar cases to wrangle, so they're off the hook, but the rest of us get lumbered with various bits of the broken-up drum kit, which has been hastily bundled up in blankets and bin bags held together with packing tape.

The train is stuffed with office workers headed to

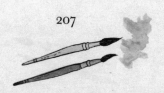

Birmingham; they eye us with disgust, and there's no way we can battle our way through the carriage to find seats. We stick together near the doors, where anyone getting on or off has to shove past us amid much swearing and sharp elbow jabs.

Bobbi-Jo gets on at Brookleigh, barging her way on to the train using her keyboard case as a battering ram.

'Careful,' I say, edging backwards and bumping into Romy, who is clutching her violin case and looking hot, bothered and miserable. 'Sorry, Romy!'

Bobbi-Jo shoves past a red-faced businessman who has somehow found himself stuck in the crowd of teenage musicians. Lexie fails to get her plastic-wrapped hi-hat stand and cymbals out of the way in time, and accidentally prods Bobbi-Jo in the ribs before dropping the whole thing on the businessman's shiny shoes. He grimaces, looking as if he'd like to be anywhere but here. He's not the only one.

'Ouch!' Bobbi-Jo shrieks, doubling up as though she's been stabbed. 'I bet that's going to bruise!'

Lexie gets tangled up in a rush of apologies, but Bobbi-Jo is having none of it. 'Look, Lexie – just because you're not with Marley any more, don't get violent, OK?'

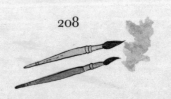

'Violent?' Lexie protests. 'Are you kidding? It was an accident!'

'Of course it was,' I argue, trying to calm things down a bit. 'This train is like a sardine can – nobody has room to move. Lexie didn't mean to hurt you.'

'You reckon?' Bobbi-Jo snarls. 'Dream on, Sami. Jealousy is not a nice thing!'

'Huh? Why would I be jealous?' Lexie asks. 'And who exactly am I supposed to be jealous of?'

'Me, obviously,' the other girl snaps. 'Because now that I'm in the band, Marley confides in me instead of you. We talk through plans together. We share a vision.'

I'm not sure what the vision is, but I'm willing to bet it's more about fame, fortune and power than anything to do with the actual music. Bobbi-Jo is clearly in a foul mood, but typically Lexie doesn't rise to the bait.

'That's great,' she says. 'I'm happy for you!'

'Oh, really?' Bobbi-Jo retorts, smug and snarly at the same time. 'Of course you're not. Drop the sickly-sweet act – it's not fooling anyone! You're green with envy because Marley's with me now! We're together, OK?'

Over by the opposite door I see Marley look across,

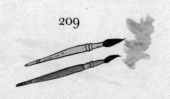

catching the mention of his name, straining to hear what's being said.

'You're actually going out with Marley?' Lexie says.

'Well, duh!' she snaps. 'That's what I said, isn't it?'

Lexie, Romy and I exchange baffled glances.

'So . . . he's not gay any more?' Romy blurts out. 'Really? Wow!'

'Gay?' Bobbi-Jo echoes. 'Of course he's not! Tell her, Lexie!'

Lexie blinks. Two spots of colour bloom in her cheeks, but she's trapped in Bobbi-Jo's glare, with no escape possible. 'Um, actually I think you'll find he is,' she says.

Bobbi-Jo looks so furious that even the red-faced businessman tries to back away in alarm.

'*Marley!*' Bobbi-Jo shrieks. 'Come over here now! *Marley!*'

Marley pushes his way through the crowd, his guitar case jabbing everyone in his path. His face appears over the businessman's shoulder, grinning.

'Someone called?' he says. 'What's up?'

'I can't say it,' Bobbi-Jo whimpers. 'Romy and Lexie, they accused you . . . They said . . . Oh, it's horrible!'

'What is?'

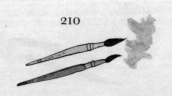

'This young lady asked if you were still gay,' the businessman reports. 'And the other young lady said of course you were. The question is, Marley, are you? Or not?'

The businessman tilts his head to one side as if trying to guess. I think he probably sees us as a particularly dodgy form of sideshow entertainment, but one he can't quite resist. 'Well?' he prompts.

'Of course I am!' Marley says. 'I was, um, planning to mention it, Bobbi-Jo. Eventually. So nobody is accusing me of anything. And it's not horrible either. It's just the way I am!'

Bobbi-Jo looks horrified, as if Marley has just announced he likes to eat worms for a hobby. 'You're kidding me?' she says. 'I mean, I thought . . . I thought we had something! All those extra keyboard lessons; all that planning for the band. I thought you were special, Marley Hayes!'

'I kind of am,' Marley says, smirking.

'Marley!' Lexie says. 'Stop being an idiot for once in your life!'

A sudden quiet falls all around us. Every member of the Lost & Found is watching now, waiting to see how this will unfold.

'It's true, isn't it?' Bobbi-Jo says. 'And everyone knew except me!'

Marley sighs. 'Look, I'm sorry if you got the wrong idea. If I've been a bit flirty . . . well, it's just the way I am. I'll flirt with anybody!'

He throws an exaggerated wink at the red-faced businessman, who grunts and turns a fetching shade of purple.

'I'm just trying to show that I don't mean anything by it,' Marley explains. 'We're friends, right, Bobbi-Jo? I can't think when I've ever said anything that might make you think otherwise.'

'It's just . . . I thought you liked me,' she whispers. 'And now, well, everyone's laughing at me!'

'Nobody's laughing,' Lexie promises, but Bobbi-Jo ignores her.

'I told my dad we were dating!' she exclaims. 'I begged him to sort the studio time. I wish I hadn't bothered, because nobody in this stupid band cares one bit about me!'

'We do care!' a handful of voices protest: Happi, Lexie, Sasha, George and Romy. It's not enough for Bobbi-Jo.

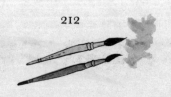

'Yeah, right,' she snaps. 'Well, guess what? I don't! I never wanted to be in your poxy band anyway. All those soppy, wimpy songs and slit-your-wrist violin solos. I've never seen a bigger bunch of misfits in my whole life! You were just using me for my looks and my keyboard skills.'

There's a snort of muffled laughter from the back of the crowded carriage as Lee and Bex struggle to keep straight faces.

'And you, Marley,' Bobbi-Jo goes on. 'You're supposed to be coming to supper later to meet my mum and talk about making a video for the new single.'

'I can still do that!' Marley says brightly.

'Over my dead body,' she snaps.

A stony silence descends.

Bobbi-Jo takes out her mobile and starts texting furiously, while the rest of us clutch our drum-kit parcels and exchange anxious looks.

The red-faced businessman loosens his tie. 'It's going to be a scorcher again today,' he announces, to nobody in particular. 'These trains could do with air conditioning, don't you think?'

'I am sick of this stupid band,' Bobbi-Jo declares, still

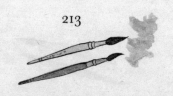

texting, and I think that the businessman is sick of it too, and sick of having the neck of a guitar jabbing into his side and sick of being hemmed in by teenagers and random bits of drum kit and stuck in the middle of a row. I am almost certain he is planning to take an earlier train to work tomorrow, or possibly call in sick with some stress-related ailment. Who could blame him?

At last the train pulls into Birmingham New Street and everyone spills out on to the platform. Bobbi-Jo dumps the keyboard case on the platform and marches off towards the escalators.

'So, um, what's happening?' Dylan asks. 'Are we doing this thing or not?'

'Of course we are,' Marley tells us. 'Wait up, Bobbi-Jo! You've forgotten your keyboard!'

For a moment, I think that Bobbi-Jo will ignore him and go on walking, but she stops and turns to face us, eyes flashing anger.

'Not my circus, not my monkey,' she quips. 'I won't be needing it any more. The stupid thing's out of tune anyway.'

'How would you know?' Lee mutters.

'Shhh,' Marley says. 'C'mon, Bobbi-Jo, there's no need

to make a big thing of this. We need you. You're our keyboardist, plus you're the only one who knows where this studio is! We've got a single to record, right?'

'Wrong, Marley Hayes,' she says. 'No single, no studio time, no video, no nothing. I've just texted Dad and he's cancelled it all. I'm going to catch a train back to Millford now, because I have an important meeting with T-Dawg and Pretty Street about joining their band. At least they appreciate me. So long, losers!'

She waggles her fingers, then turns on her sparkly wedge-heeled sandals and stalks away.

By the time we got to Austria, things were falling apart. Joe got sick and although the charity volunteers managed to get him to a hospital his rattling cough turned into pneumonia. We waited outside for him for three days, the kids and me, our little dome tent pitched on the grass at the edge of the hospital grounds.

On the third day I went in to see him with a handful of Coke-can stars I'd made from thrown-away tins, but Joe's bed was empty. His journey had ended there, alone in an Austrian hospital with nobody to hold his hand as he gave up the fight. Nazz vanished a few days later — nobody knew where he'd gone. Amira was silent after that. She stopped singing, stopped dancing.

Getting to London no longer seemed possible. We'd heard rumours about the Jungle camp at Calais — it was supposed to be wild, dangerous, a kind of refugee war zone, always under threat of being shut down. No place for children, everybody told me. Was it fair to take a bunch of little kids all that way when there was no guarantee we'd get any further?

In the end, I decided to travel with a group of students heading for the Italian border, and the kids, as always, followed me. I played my flute and Amira hung on to my coat-tails, literally, the others following behind. Step by step, we walked towards another border.

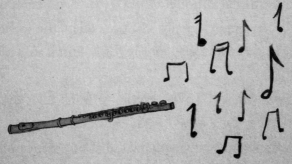

21

Making the Best of Things

Marley sinks down on to the station platform, legs crossed, head in hands. He looks as though he might cry.

'Mate,' I say, touching his shoulder. 'It'll be OK. It's not the end of the world!'

'How would you know?' Marley mutters, and I have to laugh, because, although Bobbi-Jo's departure is bad news for the band, it really isn't the end of the world. I've seen what that looks like, more or less, and it was nothing like this.

'C'mon, Marley,' Lexie coaxes. 'I didn't take you for a quitter! We're here now – what do we do?'

Bex prods him gently with the toe of one shiny pink Doc

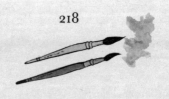

Marten boot. 'You made a mistake,' she says. 'So what? I've made a million. Won't be the first time, won't be the last.'

Marley looks up. 'Just don't you dare say "I told you so!"' he growls, and Bex laughs.

'As if,' she teases. 'Why would I? It's much more fun to watch you beating yourself up! Get up, idiot. I think we need breakfast and a new plan . . .'

Half an hour later, we're holed up in a little cafe just round the corner from New Street station, drinking orange juice and crunching through mounds of toast and jam, our instruments piled up around us. This cheers us all up, even Marley; the loss of promised studio time and the chance to record our first single seems a little less painful.

'I'm really, really sorry,' Romy says for the hundredth time. 'I got confused. Bobbi-Jo was winding me up. I really didn't mean to drop you in it, Marley!'

'My fault,' Marley says. 'I thought I had it all sorted, but you lot were right. I was kidding myself, playing stupid games. I knew Bobbi-Jo fancied me a bit – well, obviously, who wouldn't?'

'I wouldn't,' Bex snaps, throwing a toast crust at him.

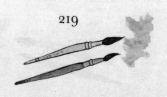

'Not if you were the last boy on the planet. You are the vainest, most arrogant and ridiculous boy I have ever met!'

'I love you too,' Marley quips, biting into the toast. 'I know I've messed up, let you all down – I thought that having Bobbi-Jo on board would open new doors for us. I didn't bank on her being tone deaf, or having a crush on me. I wanted to tell her I was gay, but I didn't want to upset her.'

'I'd say you failed on that one,' Lexie points out. 'Still, it's water under the bridge now. We've lost an opportunity – but I'm actually kind of glad.'

'I reckon we'd have been in even more trouble if everything had gone to plan and the single had been released,' Dylan says. 'What's the use of putting a single out when we all know we've lost our spark? We need to get back to basics!'

'Like how?' Marley frowns.

'Playing live, writing new songs and working together to give them that special sound,' Lexie suggests. 'That's what I miss. It's been all tense and stressy lately. We need to bring the fun back!'

'It's not that easy.' Marley says, scowling.

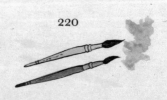

'It could be,' Bex says. 'If you'd just listen to the rest of us occasionally. We need to work as a team. Don't just assume you know best – you clearly don't. We're not just some glorified backing band for your meteoric rise to fame, y'know!'

Marley sighs. 'I know. I'm sorry. I've let you down, dragged you here on a wasted journey . . .'

Bex grins. 'Nope!' she says. 'It's only a wasted day if we don't make the most of the opportunity. We're here, in one of the UK's biggest, busiest cities, and we have all our instruments. Why not set up and play? Get some practice, have some fun, maybe earn enough to cover the cost of our train fare and our breakfast?'

Marley blinks. 'Play where?' he asks.

'Anywhere,' Bex says. 'Everywhere! I've just texted Jake and he's on his way over with a couple of busking amps and two mics. Nice and simple. We can play those summer covers you've brainwashed us with. Lord knows, we've practised them enough, and they're the perfect set list for a day like this! C'mon, Marley – let's get out there and make a mark on this place. Unless you've got any better suggestions?'

221

'I . . . well, no,' Marley says. 'That's the best idea I've heard in weeks!'

Before long, we're set up on the corner of the High Street. Dylan finds a plastic beer crate to sit on to play the drums, and then Jake appears with the mics and busking amps, and we're in business. It feels quite strange to set up our kit in the street, with passing shoppers eyeing us curiously, but the moment we start to play the shyness evaporates.

We're playing for the fun of it, and Bex is right – it gives us an edge, a buzz. Sasha sets up the keyboard and plays while she sings, the way she did before Bobbi-Jo appeared, and the difference is huge – turns out it's easy to play when you don't have constant earache. After all we've been through with Bobbi-Jo, it looks like we had the perfect keyboard player in the band the whole time.

After the first couple of songs, we relax into it, jamming on Marley's summer covers playlist to grab the attention of the punters and slipping the occasional original in among them. Slowly at first, coins and even paper notes are thrown into Marley's guitar case. We're making money in the sunshine, doing something we love.

At half eleven we take a break, drink ice-cold smoothies and move on towards the Bullring where we find an even better pitch. We're already in profit, and that's after the breakfast bill and the cost of the smoothies has been deducted. We work our way through the summer playlist again, and this time a small crowd gathers to watch and listen.

Buzzed and elated, the band seem to be taking Bobbi-Jo's advice about getting some dance moves out there too. Marley and Sasha have evolved a cute little wiggle-and-bump routine, Romy and Lexie are belting out the harmonies with added shimmies as they sing, and Lee gets everyone whistling and whooping as he breaks into a crazy, gawky, jazzy stomp to accompany his trumpet solos. Lexie turns to me and sings a snippet of 'Walking on Sunshine' at me, the two of us grinning and improvising a dance of our own that ends up with a jokey, exaggerated jive. It feels like the band is back on track – the fun's definitely back, anyway, and the crowd love it, getting out their phones to record us.

We launch into our version of 'Dancing in the Street', and every single one of us is on a high. If you'd told me two years ago I'd be clowning around playing flute with a bunch of British kids while people made videos and threw money, I'd never have believed it. It's like I've shed whole layers of sadness along with my father's coat. I'm learning to be happy again.

There were helpers all along the way, from the volunteers who pulled me out of the sea in Kos to those offering soup or sandwiches or medical support to anyone in need, but as we crossed the Italian border things changed. The charity workers saw our group for what it was, a bunch of kids adrift and lost in the middle of the biggest exodus of the twenty-first century. We were unaccompanied minors, according to the law, and one charity, Footsteps to Freedom, said they could help us.

We were given accommodation in a house, not tents. We were given hot food, books, counselling and warm clothes, because winter was coming again. I was weary by then, but I allowed myself to hope that we might make it through. I allowed myself to dream.

And then Amira got ill, felled by a flu bug sweeping through the camp. She was so small, so thin, so weak. She didn't stand a chance. I wanted to give up myself then. I had no more fight, no more hope. I just wanted it all to end.

Then I met a woman called Sally from Footsteps to Freedom.

'Do you have any relatives in Europe?' she asked. 'Anyone who could help you?'

'I have an aunt and uncle,' I told her. 'They have a tailor's shop in London, I think. Or somewhere. I don't have their address – we lost touch, but my mother was born in Britain. She was a British citizen. Her brother Dara lives there still.'

Sally raised an eyebrow and smiled. 'I think we can help you,' she said. 'Sami, if it's humanly possible, we will get you to your family.'

22

A Message from the Past

The money rains into Marley's guitar case. Little kids are bopping around in front of us, their mums taking photos. Jake makes a sign with the band's name written in black Sharpie pen, with our Facebook, Twitter and Instagram links.

We break again at two to sit in the shade and eat sandwiches and ice cream, and then it's back to work for the last part of the afternoon, big smiles on our faces. As we're delivering a truly blistering version of 'School's Out', I catch sight of a familiar face in the crowd. Soumia, our ex keyboard player, is standing watching, arms linked with an older girl in a sparkly white hijab who is almost certainly her sister.

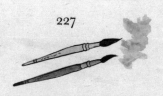

We wave and grin, and Marley dedicates our Beatles cover, 'Here Comes the Sun', to Soumia. She holds up her mobile, recording it, and when that song ends Sasha steps forward and tells the crowd that we're switching styles a little to sing one of our originals, 'Song for the Sea', inspired by the refugee crisis in Europe. She doesn't mention me, and I am grateful for that.

The crowd are silent as Jake's sample of crashing waves begins to play. George does his cello piece and I come in with my flute solo, and this time Sasha takes her cue right on time. Her voice is cool and clear and haunting, and when Romy and Lexie join in with their heartbreaking harmonies there's a different kind of buzz going on.

We have the audience in the palm of our hand, and we know it.

When the last soaring violin notes fade away, you can hear a pin drop, and then the crowd erupt into riotous applause. Soumia, smiling from a distance, films the whole thing.

It's late when we get back to Millford. We were loud and happy on the train, full of celebratory pizza and fizzy drinks

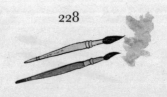

as well as the thrill of success. Now, as we carry the equipment back to the old railway carriage, the talk is all about a future that suddenly seems hopeful again.

'Today didn't quite go to plan,' Marley is saying. 'But I'm glad! Sometimes fate knows best, huh?'

'And fate decreed that after weeks of trying to get you to dump Bobbi-Jo, she dumped us,' Lee comments. 'Oh, the irony!'

'You were right, though,' Marley admits. 'She couldn't play. Not at all. She was so bad that at times I thought she was doing it on purpose.'

'And, boy, did she fancy you!' Bex says. 'There really is no accounting for taste!'

'I bet she's joined Pretty Street by now, y'know,' Jake says. 'It might be more her thing, anyway – what did they want her to do? Dancing and backing vocals?'

'She might be OK at that,' Sasha concedes.

'She's the kind of girl who always lands on her feet,' Lexie says. 'I think she'll be OK. I hope so.'

'She will, and so will the Lost & Found now,' Marley declares. 'Playing live is what we do best. How did I ever forget that? We've got something special – today proved it.

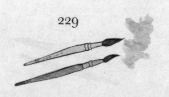

I've messed up, made some mistakes, I know that. We lost our way for a little while, but I think we've found it again!'

'Deep,' Bex teases. 'Lost & Found on the streets of Birmingham, huh?'

'We're much more than a busking band, obviously,' Marley states. 'But . . . well, today was pretty cool.'

'Don't knock it,' Bex says. 'We've paid our train fares, had breakfast, lunch and tea, bought cold drinks and ice cream and suncream and we've still got some left over. Has anyone checked our social media?'

'Fifty-three new likes on our Facebook page, over a hundred new followers on Twitter and loads of new followers on Instagram too,' Happi reports. 'And Soumia's put that video of "Song for the Sea" up on our Facebook page too – it's getting loads of views and shares! Not bad for a day's work!'

'Not bad at all,' Marley grins. 'I've learned my lesson. We're a team, and we work together. Any big decisions, we all get a say. I think we can safely say we've got our spark back!'

I feel so happy I barely notice the walk home. My head's in the clouds, my heart daring to hope again.

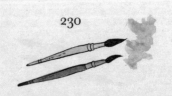

That Arctic summer . . . I keep forgetting that it can't go on forever.

'Where were you last night? Aunt Zenna scolds at breakfast. 'I waited up till past eleven!'

'Sorry, Aunt Zenna,' I say. 'I should have called. We went busking in Birmingham, then had a pizza together. I lost track of time!'

She sighs. 'Let me know next time you're going to be home late,' she tells me. 'I worry, Sami! Anyway, this parcel came for you.'

She pushes a small, lumpy package across the table towards me, and I know at once it is the charger I ordered online for my father's phone. Suddenly, I want nothing more than to leave that voicemail, tell my father I made it, reached Britain, found Uncle Dara and Aunt Zenna. I want to tell him I'm playing in a band, drawing again, looking for silver linings. I want to tell him about Lexie.

I go back to my bedroom and take out the phone, plug it in. I have no idea if it will take a charge – perhaps it just won't be possible to revive it after all this time. I have to try, though.

At first, there is no sign of life, but, five minutes on, the

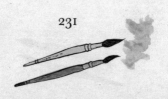

phone buzzes softly and the screen lights up, showing a battery symbol with the tiniest sliver of red. My heart leaps.

I force myself to sit still, to sew a few bits of treasure into the lining of the old overcoat. It's almost finished, and I'm trying to pluck up the courage to show it to Lexie and possibly also Louisa Winter. I need to know if they think it's crazy or, possibly, cool. With invisible stitches I attach a couple of magpie feathers found in the park yesterday, blue-black and silver white, then slide the coat back on to its hanger and check my own phone. There's a message from Lexie telling me to look on the Lost & Found Facebook page because Soumia's video is going crazy.

I click through to the band's page and there is the clip of us performing 'Song for the Sea'. When I look more closely, I see that the video has been shared over three hundred times and has had more than ten thousand views. It is going viral. I know that when Marley sees this he'll practically explode, and I laugh out loud, riding an adrenaline rush, because this is way better than any single could have been. Our song, out there on the internet, maybe raising awareness and making people think . . . It's kind of awesome.

I go back to check my father's mobile. Now the red stripe is wider, and when I swipe the screen, the home page appears. I click on the phone icon, ready to leave my message, and that's when I see it: the little red marker that says there are five unread voicemails.

The breath catches in my throat.

I pull the mobile free, click on to the oldest voicemail message and press play. Suddenly the world falls away.

I hear my mother's voice, tearful and panicked. The words are Kurdish, the words we spoke at home, between ourselves. They seem distant and unfamiliar to my ears now.

'Karim, are you there?' my mother says. 'Please call me back on this number, tell me that you and Sami are safe. Roza and I were picked up by a fishing boat and taken to a small island called Ios. We are OK, but we cannot stay here and I'm frightened, Karim. I don't know what to do. Call me, please, as soon as you get this message –'

Abruptly, the voicemail ends and the screen goes black; the battery is dead again. The phone slips through my shaking fingers and on to the floor.

These were the messages from my mother.

> Karim, are you there? Please call me back on this number, tell me that you and Sami are safe. Roza and I were picked up by a fishing boat and taken to a small island called Ios. We are OK, but we cannot stay here and I'm frightened, Karim. I don't know what to do. Call me, please, as soon as you get this message . . . ask to speak to Ali. He will get a message to me.

> Please call me back on this number, Karim. I need to know that you and Sami are safe. Roza and I are staying for the moment in a small house on the coast, sharing with another family from Syria – this is Ali's mobile. His wife, Maria, is Spanish, and they have three daughters, one the same age as Roza. The family are paying one of the fishermen to take them to Spain. They say they will take us also, but I cannot go without you, Karim, without Sami . . .

We have waited three weeks and there has been no word. My friends say we must face the truth, accept that we are alone now. We cannot stay here, and they say we have a much better chance in Spain than trying to get to mainland Greece and making the journey across Europe on foot. The boat is quite a big one, and the fisherman is kind and well used to such trips. He says we must leave very soon, before the weather turns, but I do not want to believe that I have lost you, Karim, lost my Sami. I think my heart will break. Should I go to Spain? Should I wait? Please call!

I know you will not hear me, Karim. I know in my heart that you are not listening, but still I cannot give up hope. I want to tell you that Roza and I are in Spain now, in a town called Malaga, a busy city where we can pass unnoticed. Ali and Maria have arranged false papers for us, so I can work, but I am afraid every day that someone will find out we are not supposed to be here. We have new names. We are illegal. How can that be? How can a human being be illegal? Oh, Karim, I wish we were all together. You would know what to do.

This will be my last message, Karim. I need to let go of the past and move on. Sometimes I dream of the life we hoped for in London. It seemed so impossible, but I should have listened, Karim, I should have trusted you. We could have been there now. Without you and Sami, what is the point? I do not have the strength to travel on to Britain – not now, perhaps not ever. Roza and I are safe here, we have rooms to live in, enough money to buy food and clothes. Roza goes to school every day and is almost fluent now in Spanish. In my heart I know that you would find me if you could, but I cannot bring myself to give up hope. I will wait for you both. I love you both, always.

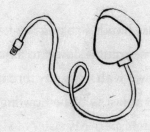

23

A Boat to Spain

Someone is howling, a harsh, guttural sound that seems to tear the air apart. I am on my knees on the bedroom floor, hunched over, stabbing at my father's phone with one finger, but it's dead, dead, dead.

'Sami, Sami, what is it?' Aunt Zenna is saying. 'What's happened? Are you sick?'

'Where does it hurt, Sami?' my uncle's voice asks, and I want to tell him that it hurts everywhere: in my heart, in my soul, in every single cell of my body, but I cannot seem to find the words. Still the howling goes on, and after a while I become aware of my uncle's strong arms around me, my aunt's cool hands stroking the hair back from my brow, and the noise softens slowly to a quiet sob.

My cheeks are wet with tears, my throat raw with crying, and I understand at last that the howling was me.

'My mother,' I whisper. 'My sister . . . I think, maybe . . . maybe they're still alive.'

The world turns upside down. I lose track of time, lose track of everything. I am anchored only to the past, but I am not alone with it as I was once. My social worker Ben appears, a frown of concern crumpling his brow. He listens to the voicemails, talks to my aunt and uncle, makes endless calls on his own mobile. 'We must not get our hopes up,' he tells us. 'These messages were sent, what, two years ago? Three?'

'The first message dates from just after the wreck – so, yes, three years ago,' I say. 'The last message, a year and a half, I think.'

'We have never had a case like this,' Ben says. 'It's unheard of. We've sent for a Kurdish translator – once we have an official transcript of the messages, we can move forward.'

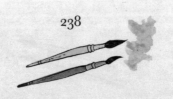

'You'll call the number?' Uncle Dara asks. 'We have to know if my sister and my niece are alive! My sister is a British citizen – please, help us to find her!'

'We'll do everything we can,' Ben says. 'It may take time – it is important to go through the proper channels. Finding missing persons – refugees – in mainland Europe . . . well, it can be a little like looking for a needle in a haystack, as you can imagine. We will do all we can, Sami, I promise you.'

He shakes my uncle by the hand and claps me on the back awkwardly, before leaving the flat. He doesn't seem to understand that I'm sick with fear and longing, that I can't eat, can't speak, can't even think. All this time I had my father's mobile phone, and not once before now had I tried to find a charger for it. If I had, I'd have known that my mother and sister had survived the wreck. If only, if only, if only.

At some point, I remember I'm supposed to be meeting Lexie, and send her a message to cancel.

Sami: I'm not going to make the park today. Everything's gone crazy.

239

I charged my dad's old mobile like we talked about and there were FIVE messages from my mum. I think my mum and sister might be alive! x

Lexi: OMG! Sami! For real? xoxo

Sami: For real. Can't believe it. Feel numb. Can you tell Marley I won't be at practice? Can't think straight! x

Lexi: Have messaged the others, don't worry about anything. This is amazing, Sami. BEYOND amazing. Can I come over? xoxo

Sami: Sure. This waiting for news is driving me mad. Think I'm in shock. Can't get my head around it. See you soon. x

One by one my friends appear – Marley swears and tells me not to worry if I have to miss a couple of rehearsals; Bex growls and tells me that miracles do happen; Happi brings cupcakes and the promise that she'll pray for my family to be found. They each stay a while, drink Aunt Zenna's sweet treacly coffee, and leave again. The others message me good-luck wishes and ask if there's anything they can do, but there's nothing anyone can do, of course. Nothing at all.

Then Lexie comes, bringing no gifts, no promises, just a small tortoise in a cardboard carrying case. She puts her arms around me and I rest my head on her shoulder.

'What if they are alive, Lexie?' I whisper.

'If they're out there, they'll be found,' Lexie says. 'You have social services on your side. They'll know what to do, who to contact.'

'My social worker says it will take time,' I tell her. 'He says it's like looking for a needle in a haystack. They don't seem to understand that I've waited forever already . . . I don't think I can be patient! Over a year since the last message – anything could have happened.'

'They'll be found,' she repeats. 'Oh, Sami, it's the saddest story – but I think there'll be a happy ending!'

I know this must be hard for Lexie; she carries the hurt of her own loss too, after all, yet there is no anger, no envy in her. We curl up together on the sofa, Mary Shelley roaming across the carpet, and my aunt forgets her prim and proper ways and smiles benevolently as if the little tortoise is an honoured guest. Well, she is, I guess.

As for Lexie, my Aunt Zenna practically hugs her to death.

The Kurdish translator comes to make a transcript of the messages, then goes away again. Jake calls to tell me that Louisa Winter has called Footsteps to Freedom to see if they can help me, and to pass on the message that I am not alone.

'I can't stand this,' I groan. 'It's driving me mad. Are they still in Spain? Did they try to come to Britain? I have to know!'

'Your mother is a British citizen,' Aunt Zenna says. 'She and Roza would be safe and legal here. But wouldn't she have found us by now?'

I frown. We had no address for my uncle and aunt because my grandfather had disowned them and thrown away their letters. Thanks to the tall stories my grandfather liked to tell, we'd believed they lived in London, when actually they were in Millford all along. Footsteps to Freedom had traced them in the end, but it took a long time.

'You just have to wait,' Lexie says. 'See if the powers that be can track them down.'

And that's it, really. I feel helpless, in limbo, waiting for social services or the government or Footsteps to Freedom – someone, anyone – to do something.

I blink, my heart thumping, and scramble to my feet.

'What if I don't wait?' I say, my voice shaking. 'What if I do what my mother asked, and ring the number she gave me? If someone answers – anyone – they'll know where she is, surely?'

'Sami, no!' my aunt cries when she sees me grab up the mobile phone. 'What if you hear something you don't want to hear? We should wait, do as we've been told!'

'Do you think I don't fear the worst already?' I fling back at her. 'I believed that they were dead, Aunt Zenna, until this morning. I have to do this. And, besides, they didn't tell us not to ring . . .'

I see hope flash across her face, watch my uncle rise from

the kitchen table where he has been altering a three-piece suit.

I click on the first voicemail, write down the number that left the message, and call it from my phone. There's a strange beeping noise, and then a woman's voice speaking in Spanish.

'Can I please speak to Yasmine Tagara?' I ask in English, then switch to Kurdish and finally Arabic. 'Please? Do you know her? Do you know my mother?'

There is silence at the other end of the phone, and then the voice says, in Arabic this time, 'You are Yasmine's son? Samir?'

If Lexie and Aunt Zenna weren't holding me up I think I would fall, but I manage to stay upright. 'Yes, this is Samir,' I say. 'Is it possible to speak to my mother?'

There is another silence, and I can't tell if it's because I am calling Spain and there's some kind of time lapse, or if it's something worse.

'Samir,' the woman says. 'Yasmine and Roza are no longer here. They flew to Britain a month ago. They're living on the south coast, awaiting assessment.'

Setting Sun

I could take a boat to Spain
I could change my name
So it sounds like something new
And when all is like the setting sun
Let me sing this song for you

The map held all our dreams
Our nightmares, so it seems
I'm going back to where it all began
When the moon is full
I'm a passing bird
Fly with me if you can

Somewhere out in this world
You'll find your perfect girl
I could tell you that it was me
We could dance like stars
Across the sky
If I could only make you see

So I took that boat to Spain
I changed, oh I changed my name
Now I've become someone new
And all is like the setting sun
But where, oh where, are you?

24

The Beach

There is one thing left to tick off our list of dates: a trip to the beach. I didn't think I'd ever want to see the sea again, but Lexie says the English Channel is very different from the Aegean Sea, that the British seaside is something that everyone has to experience at least once.

We're on the train, Lexie and me, with Mary Shelley on the seat between us in her cardboard carrying case, the top part open so she can peek out. Any chance of romance is squashed flat by the presence of my aunt and uncle, sitting just across the aisle, sharing a puzzle book and eating baklava.

'You OK?' Lexie asks me.

'Sure,' I lie. 'It's just – a bit of a weird situation, that's all . . .'

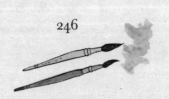

This is an understatement. I remember one winter's day in Greece when one of the older kids had found a dead rabbit by the side of the road, killed by a passing car. It'd been a long time since any of us had eaten fresh meat, and he'd been so proud of his find and determined that we'd finally have a feast. The trouble was, he had to skin and gut and clean the rabbit first. I remember the rabbit's face, calm and still and beautiful, one glassy amber eye staring blindly at the sky. I remember how the boy tried to peel off its skin like a fur glove, how he'd scowled and sworn and finally given up. I remember the stench of blood as he'd sliced along the animal's belly, pulled out the entrails in a wet, twisted tangle. He roasted the meat in the fire and claimed it was the best thing he'd ever eaten, but none of us had the heart to join him.

My guts feel like that poor rabbit's, all twisted and torn and pulled about.

Mary Shelley pokes her head out of the box, and I lift her out and sit her on my lap and let her climb up my T-shirt to look out of the train window as the world slides past in a blur. She will like the beach, even if I don't.

Lexie is playing with her mobile, checking the views on

247

our busking video. 'No way,' she says, holding out the phone for me to see. 'Two hundred thousand, three hundred and climbing . . . that's amazing! And loads of likes and shares and comments. Our Facebook page has more than ten thousand followers now – that's tripled in just a few days!'

'Wow,' I say, but my voice sounds leaden, numb. A few days ago this news would have made me elated, buzzed, on top of the world, but right now nothing matters but finding my family.

'Bobbi-Jo did us a favour, dropping us that day,' Lexie says. 'We'd never have got Marley to agree to go busking otherwise . . . and look how that turned out! Fate steps in sometimes, Sami. You have to trust that things will work out. Like now, with your mum . . .'

'What if they're not allowed to stay?' I ask.

'Your mum's a British citizen,' Lexie says. 'She has a right to be here, and Roza too. Have faith.'

She lets her head drop on to my shoulder, and we sit in silence, Mary Shelley between us, all the way to the coast.

We leave my aunt and uncle eating ice cream on a bench and head along the shore, hand in hand. We pick our way

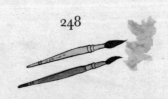

between people slumped in striped deckchairs and families loafing on fringed blankets. We kick off our shoes and carry them. I roll the cuffs of my jeans as high as they will go. We walk until the crowds thin out, drifting closer and closer to the water's edge, the incoming tide teasing our bare feet.

We stop for a while, setting Mary Shelley down on the sand. She lifts her head to sniff the air, then turns and marches away from the water, a small, determined creature, a Hermann's tortoise native to much warmer climes who has accidentally found herself on this island and plans to make the best of it. We have that much in common, Mary Shelley and I. Hard shell, soft centre, bucketloads of determination.

'I don't think she likes it,' Lexie says, and I shrug, because I don't really like it either. The past's long shadow throws a chill over everything, even this day that in different circumstances could have been fun, an adventure involving candyfloss and fish 'n' chips. Instead, it's an echo of the day I lost my father to the sea, lost my mother and my sister too. Three years on, a different place, a different beach, a different lifetime . . . maybe, just maybe, I will get my mother and my sister back.

Lexie is crouched on the beach, talking softly to Mary Shelley. I smile and walk into the waves, shivering a little at the shock of the cold water. Lexie has her back to me, following Mary Shelley on a stroll across the shore, and I turn back to the sea, the oncoming tide, feeling more alive than I have in years.

I remember crawling out of the sea on a different beach, the day my life fell apart. The sea did its best to take me, that day. It wrapped its arms around me, held me tight. Surrender, it whispered in my ear. Stay. Instead, I'd chosen to live. My hands clawed at wet, gritty sand, my face grazed against rocks as they dragged me ashore. I'd slumped on the beach and seen the sun rise as the volunteers wrapped me in blankets. I'd vomited salt water on to the sand.

In the distance, I'd heard the faint sound of bells as a trio of donkeys grazed above the shoreline, and someone singing in a language I could not understand. I'd found Europe, but lost my family. It wasn't a trade-off I would ever have chosen.

Now, I wade out further, barely aware of the water soaking my jeans, splashing up to stain my T-shirt. The further I go from the shore, the wilder the sea seems:

pushing, shoving, calling. I remember how heavy my limbs had felt that day, how the coldness had seeped right through to my bones. I remember thinking how much easier it would be to stop fighting, stop swimming, let go.

'Sami!' Lexie's voice cuts into my thoughts, and I stop abruptly, shocked at how far I've waded. Lexie seems distant, unreachable and I can taste salt on my lips once more.

'Sami! C'mon!' she yells, and I flounder back through the waves to lift her up and whirl her round and round, the two of us laughing. And then we're kissing, and although the kiss tastes of salt and shadows it also tastes of sunshine and hope and happiness.

'Time to go,' Lexie says, checking her phone. 'Two o'clock, they said, by the pier. We don't want to be late!'

I don't want to be late, of course – I have waited three years for this. Lexie scoops up Mary Shelley and puts her into the travelling case. She links hands with me as we head back along the shoreline.

'Looks like we finished the list,' I say a little sadly. 'Finally. And school starts again on Monday . . . Summer's over.'

'Summer's over, but we're just beginning, Sami,' Lexie says. 'We'll make another list. A hundred dates. A thousand!'

'We will,' I promise. 'Thanks for coming today. I hate that something that feels so wonderful for me must be so painful for you.'

Lexie shakes her head. 'Nope, not painful,' she says. 'I'm happy for you, I really am. I just hope . . .'

Her voice fades away to nothing. 'Sami,' she whispers. 'Do you think . . .?'

I look up, frowning, and I see what Lexie has seen. Two figures are walking towards us along the beach, both small and slender, both dressed simply in jeans and T-shirts, with the same dark curls and olive skin. I would know my mother and my sister anywhere.

My mother's hair is streaked with grey and clipped up in a messy bun, her face criss-crossed with worry lines. She's wearing a faded green scarf printed with roses, the fringing matted and straggly. Roza is no longer the little kid I remember; she must be twelve now, just a year younger than Lexie. She looks so grown up, so beautiful.

All four of us have stopped, wordless, staring, and I'm aware of Lexie letting go of my hand, stepping back.

'Samir? Is it really you?' my mother asks in Kurdish, her grey eyes wide. 'After all this time?'

And then I'm running towards them, laughing, and my mother wraps her arms around me, pulls Roza in too. We cling together like the pieces of a complicated puzzle that have finally slotted together, just when you'd given up hope of working out how they might fit. I breathe in the scent of lemons and vanilla I remember so well from my childhood, the smell of my mother, and my T-shirt is wet with her tears.

'So tall!' my mother says, switching to English, stroking my face, pushing the bird's-nest curls out of my eyes. 'So handsome! Not my little boy any more, but a young man! I cannot believe you're real!'

'I'm real,' I promise.

'This is Lexie,' I say, stepping back at last to slide an arm around her waist and bring her forward. 'My girlfriend. And Mary Shelley the tortoise . . .'

Lexie lifts the little tortoise out of her carrying case, and Roza squeals and steps forward to stroke Mary Shelley. My mother folds Lexie into a brief hug before glancing anxiously beyond her to where my aunt and uncle and a bearded man, who must be the bloke from Footsteps to Freedom, are now approaching.

'OK,' I say. 'You probably know . . . or maybe not – this is Uncle Dara and Aunt Zenna, and the man from the charity who is helping us!'

Everybody looks hopeful, cautious; everybody is smiling.

'Little sister,' my uncle says, and his face is wet with tears. 'Yasmine! I am so very glad you're safe. And, Roza, my niece – I am so glad you are here!'

'Dara,' my mother whispers. 'My brother! You . . . you haven't changed!'

They start to laugh. There will be lots of talking to do, lots of reconciliation and explanation. Past hurts and misunderstandings will be put aside, because blood is thicker than water and love wins over fear and pride. It will all work out. We have all the time in the world to see that it does.

'Roza,' I say, falling into step beside my sister. 'I don't know if you remember? I made this for you . . .'

I open my palm and offer her a Coke-can star. Her face breaks into the familiar grin I thought I had forgotten, then she flings her arms around me and holds on tight.

It wasn't until the following spring that I finally made it to Millford, which meant I'd been travelling for pretty much two years from the day we first left Syria. I'd just turned twelve when we left and I was fourteen when I finally made it to safety with Uncle Dara and Aunt Zenna.

In that time, I learned how to be a survivor. I'd learned how to get along with the other kids, how to switch off the pain, how to stand out from the crowd just enough. The overcoat and the flute had kept me safe, and my frozen heart kept the hurt at bay.

Millford wasn't quite what I was expecting, but I was glad to be there all the same. I went to school, joined the library, worked on my art and my English. I joined the Lost & Found, made friends, met Lexie — the girl who lit up my days with hope and possibility long before I even dared to speak to her.

When I looked up on a clear night, above the orange glow of the street lights, sometimes I could see the same stars I'd once looked at back home in Syria. I could almost imagine my father reaching up, pretending to pluck one from the sky to give to my little sister. Almost.

25

A Haircut, Maybe

The lady from the charity shop next door tells us that a barely worn blazer for Millford Park Academy has come in that might fit me, and so I go to school on the first day of the autumn term in perfect uniform.

'Wonderful!' Mr Simpson the head teacher says. 'No more overcoat!'

He squints at my hair, which is collar length now and so bushy it could easily be sheltering a small family of mice. 'Maybe a haircut next?'

'Maybe not,' I say politely, and Mr Simpson shrugs and lets me carry on my way.

Nobody else comments on the missing coat, but they all

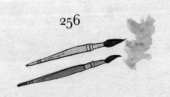

ask about the Lost & Found. Loads of kids have seen the busking video. Their parents have seen it too, and someone says it's even been mentioned on the radio – Barney Bright has been boasting about having us in the studio, promising he'll invite us back soon.

Some of the new Year Sevens ask Marley for his autograph, and he leans against the wall in the entrance foyer signing jotters with a Sharpie pen for a whole ten minutes, loving it.

'Five hundred thousand views and counting,' Happi reports. 'Once things go viral, there's no stopping them. It's been shared all over the world – London, New York, Paris, Berlin, Rio, Sydney, Lagos . . . We are an international success!'

'An internet sensation,' Marley quips. 'Who needs the Battle of the Bands?'

Pretty Street got their picture in the *Millford Gazette*, T-Dawg posing with his arm round Bobbi-Jo, who was wearing a minidress, a back-to-front baseball cap and weird hi-top trainers that came halfway up her tanned legs. The report says that her unusual backing vocals lend a distinctly British twist to the band, and that her dance routines are spellbinding.

'I'm glad she's with Pretty Street,' Lexie says. 'It's definitely more her style!'

'Their first single comes out next week,' Bex informs us. 'And guess who their new manager is? Oh well!'

We all know it wasn't just Bobbi-Jo's fault that she was such a bad fit for the Lost & Found – it was Marley's too. If he'd been honest with her from the start, things could have run a lot more smoothly.

A week later, my mother and my sister come to live in Millford.

In three weeks flat, Uncle Dara has converted the attic into a big bedroom for my mother, complete with Velux windows and easy chairs and an offcut of emerald-green carpet. Roza takes my cousin Faizah's old room, and everyone is happy.

My mother has been confirmed as a British citizen, and all of us now have the right to stay in Britain. Roza starts at Millford Park Academy and within days she has a group of new friends. Her English is still halting, uncertain, but that will not stop my little sister. My uncle puts a sign in the window advertising a new dressmaking service, and slowly the orders start to trickle in. My mother sits at the sewing machine in the workshop, turning cheap fabric into beautiful gowns, making magic out of nothing, the way she always used to.

'Teamwork,' my uncle exclaims, delighted.

'Families should stick together,' my mother agrees.

It hasn't taken long for old misunderstandings to be swept away – there is laughter and rolling of eyes at my grandfather's tall stories, regret at the family rift, and lots of shared memories between my mother and her brother about their childhood days.

On the afternoon of October 1st, Lexie and I race home, change out of our uniforms into our best clothes and head for the art gallery. Louisa Winter's exhibition is opening tonight at 7 p.m., and I want to get there early to see how my work has been displayed.

As promised, the words and pictures have been framed in plain white frames and hung round the walls of a small side gallery. In the centre of the room, the old overcoat is hanging, a slender bough of driftwood pushed through the sleeves so they stretch out on either side like wings. The coat stirs and sways gently, suspended from the ceiling by lengths of tough yet almost invisible fishing line that also tugs the front of the coat open to reveal the lining. It looks so different now.

Stitched on to the shoulders and along the backs of the arms are hundreds of feathers, rescued from parks and pavements, hedges, ditches – even that gritty south-coast beach. A winding line of running stitches, made from thick scarlet yarn, snakes across the coat to represent the journey I made in it.

And then you see the inside, glinting bright like treasure, a coat-shaped collage of all things silver. There is silver paper and chocolate wrapping, coils of shiny silver wire, old earrings, the paper lining from discarded cigarette packets, scraps of an aluminum can snipped into star shapes, milk-bottle tops, foil food trays, beads from a broken necklace. There is a beaten-down spoon, barbed wire, broken strings from Marley's guitar, a slender chain found in the mud in Serbia, scraps of Lurex and plastic and sequinned material, shards of broken glass and the fragments of a smashed mirror. There is a ribbon, a tassel, half a dozen pins, a short length of chain, nails, screws,

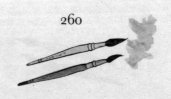

washers, the insides of an old-fashioned wristwatch. There's more, much more, and even in places a glimpse of the shiny grey satin lining my father stitched into the coat so long ago.

The coat looks as though it is flying: a tatty, beautiful, disembodied angel spinning softly in the quiet air.

Lexie tugs at my sleeve.

'It's perfect,' she whispers. 'I promise, it is. Quick, come and see the portrait – you're famous!'

We step into the foyer, where Louisa Winter has just arrived in a flurry of black silk, her vivid auburn hair piled up on her head and bound with a green silk scarf.

'Children!' she exclaims, arms stretched out to greet us. 'You're here! Have you seen your little gallery, Sami? It looks amazing! That coat!'

'It's awesome,' I say simply. 'Thank you!'

'Don't thank me,' she says, laughing. 'All the hard work was yours. I just encouraged you to share it! I expect you'd like to see the picture you modelled for too . . .'

We step into the main gallery and the painting is right in front of us, six feet tall and almost as wide. In the centre of the canvas stands a sad-faced boy in a

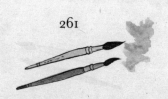

threadbare coat, playing a flute while two or three small children dance around him. His hair is wild and tangled; a small blackbird is perched on top of it. Louisa Winter's trademark is that she includes an animal in every painting she makes – I guess my bird's-nest hair has made the choice easy for her. The background of the painting is a collage of pages torn from a junk shop atlas, overpainted with trees and tents and what look like water stains. That part makes me shudder.

'It's wonderful,' I say. 'It's . . . the way it was. The way it felt. I love it!'

It's almost seven now, and the gallery is starting to fill up. The rest of the band arrive and start to set up in a corner of the lobby, ready for our set later on. Lexie's foster parents arrive, and her grandparents, and my aunt and uncle, and my mother in a moss-green dress she's made herself. Roza and a couple of her school friends are here, holding collection buckets for Footsteps to Freedom. I see Mr Simpson drop some notes in, and my art teacher and Miss Walker, the pink-haired librarian. The mayor of Millford is here, making small talk with Barney Bright, Bobbi-Jo and T-Dawg. I see the bearded man from Footsteps to

Freedom, my social worker Ben and even a couple of photographers and TV cameramen.

'Whoa,' Marley whispers, elbowing me in the ribs. 'Look! Ked Wilder!'

The legendary sixties pop star cuts through the crowd, unmistakable in his black fedora, skinny jeans and Chelsea boots. He embraces Louisa Winter and is instantly surrounded by reporters and photographers.

'Don't hassle him,' Lexie warns. 'Stay cool, Marley. Seriously.'

'But . . .'

'Lexie's right,' I tell him. 'Trust me.'

'OK,' Marley agrees. 'At least we've got a cover of his song in our set list!'

Moments later, a reporter collars me, asking how Footsteps to Freedom helped me, how I came to meet Louisa Winter and why I began to make art of my own. Across the room, I see Ms Winter and my mother talking to a TV cameraman, with the beardy guy from Footsteps to Freedom next in line to be interviewed. This isn't just an exhibition; thanks to Ms Winter, it's much, much more than that. People clump together in front of the paintings,

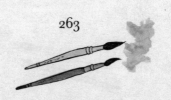

peering closely and sipping glasses of champagne. 'Iconic and powerful,' I hear the mayor say as I wander past.

My mother is harder to impress, but when she sees the art piece made from my father's coat, she cries.

'Oh, Sami,' she whispers. 'My clever, wonderful boy!'

Later, she pauses in front of Ms Winter's portrait of me, frowning. 'I like it,' she concedes. 'But, Sami, that blackbird . . . your hair! I'll make an appointment at the barber's tomorrow!'

There is only one person in the whole wide world I'd consider getting my hair cut for, and that's my mother. Maybe.

In the side gallery, a photographer is taking shot after shot of the silver lining coat. 'I always knew the coat was symbolic,' Bobbi-Jo is telling T-Dawg. 'A metaphor. Or something. A work of art . . .'

Out in the lobby, Lee blows a trumpet blast, the signal for everyone to gather for the speeches, and the foyer fills up as Louisa Winter takes the mic.

'I want to thank you all so very much for being here tonight,' she begins. 'It's a long time since I've done an exhibition. I have to admit I was very much inspired by

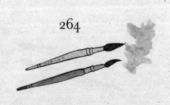

Millford's own rising stars of the music world, the Lost & Found, who practise at Greystones and will be playing for you shortly.

'When I discovered a few months ago that one of the band was a fifteen-year-old Syrian refugee, I was astonished. Sami's journey and the hardships he endured were unimaginable to me, but slowly the theme of journeys began to creep into my work. When I found out about Footsteps to Freedom, who work at grassroots level to help unaccompanied refugee children, I knew I had to help them – suddenly, the idea of an exhibition was much more appealing.

'It was only recently that I discovered that Footsteps to Freedom had helped to bring Sami to his relatives in the UK, and more recently still that I enlisted their help in reuniting Sami with the mother and sister he believed were lost. You can see some of this extraordinary young man's artwork here today . . .' She waves an arm towards the side room, a dozen bracelets jangling.

'I hope you'll take the opportunity to look and to understand, and perhaps find it in your hearts to donate. As you know, all proceeds from the paintings sold here will

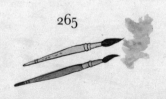

go to the charity also. Sami's is just one small story, but it has a happy ending – thanks to Footsteps to Freedom!'

The crowd erupt into loud applause, and after a short speech by the bloke from Footsteps to Freedom we take our places on the makeshift stage.

Marley takes the mic. 'Thank you, Ms Winter, for having us here tonight. We're thrilled to be part of this, not just because we love your artwork but because of my mate Sami. Who knew he was such a brilliant artist on top of his musical skills? Sami isn't just talented; he's a genuinely good guy . . . I'm proud to have him in the band and proud to call him a friend. We're going to kick off with a brand-new song inspired by Sami and his lovely family – it's called "Setting Sun".'

After weeks of practice, we are pitch perfect, and our newest song has the audience silent, transfixed. When the last violin notes fade away, the applause is deafening. We have the audience enthralled, and when our short set of original material is done, we go on playing our summer covers playlist as background music while the crowd, at Marley's request, relax and go on looking at the paintings.

As Marley announces our last cover, the classic 'Summer

Daze' by Ked Wilder, I notice the TV cameras moving closer and, without warning, Ked himself steps up to the mic to duet with Sasha in a joyful, high-energy finale.

'Ked!' Marley gasps as the last dregs of applause fall away. 'It's great to see you! We've missed you!'

'You've been working hard in my absence, I see,' the star says. 'That was a great set. Let's meet soon and make some plans, yeah? See if I can help you?'

'Yes please!' Marley says. He flings his arms around me and Lexie, then hauls in anyone else within arm's length for a messy group hug. I find myself caught in the middle, and instead of breaking away I realize that this is where I want to be, right here, in the middle of my friends.

When an Arctic summer is over, the big freeze sets in again, but I don't want to go back to that, I really don't. I'm getting used to the sunshine. I have my mother and my sister back, I have friends, and I have Lexie. I have hopes and dreams and plans for the future . . . and at last I've learned to make my own silver lining.

It was an epic journey, a terrifying journey, a journey from a broken world towards the possibility of freedom. Along the way, I lost my father, my mother, my sister. I lost my hopes and dreams, my childhood, but I found some stuff too.

I found that I was stronger than I had ever imagined, and that there was safety in numbers, in sticking together and looking out for each other. I found that even in the darkest times you can laugh and sing and play the flute, and make a silver lining from the rubbish you find on the roadside.

I found that even when I thought my heart had frozen like a stone inside me, in fact, it was still beating, still caring, still loving life. The things I had put into deep freeze were just waiting for me to be brave enough to claim them back.

Love hurts, life hurts, but both are gifts you have to hold on tight to. You cannot waste them.

And no matter how hard things get, there is always a silver lining.

Marley's Vintage Summer Playlist

★ Summertime (George Gershwin)

★ Summer in the City (The Lovin' Spoonful)

★ Here Comes the Sun (The Beatles)

★ Surfin' U.S.A (The Beach Boys)

★ Summer of '69 (Bryan Adams)

★ Dancing in the Street (Martha and the Vandellas)

★ School's Out (Alice Cooper)

★ Walking on Sunshine (Katrina and the Waves)

★ Sunshine Superman (Donovan)

★ Summer Daze (Ked Wilder)*

This one's fictional, but the others are real . . . Check them out!

Afterword

Sami's journey to the UK was fictional but it is based on real journeys that were every bit as tough. Sami and his family left Syria early on in the conflict, and life has become much harder since then for refugees fleeing to Europe. Borders have been closed, barbed wire and soldiers with tear gas have been deployed to prevent people moving across Europe, and laws have been passed to deport many refugees back to where they came from. If my fictional characters had not had relatives in the UK (or British nationality in the case of Yasmine) they may never have reached safety here, and thousands of unaccompanied children and teens are still struggling through terrifyingly dangerous situations to find somewhere they can call home.

How can we help? I am donating the advance fee for this book to refugee charities, including CRIBS International, which helps mothers and babies; and Safe Passage, which (like the fictional Footsteps to Freedom) helps unaccompanied minors to safety. Could you help too? You can also collect items of clothing to send to those on their journey – find out whether your local area has a refugee aid collection centre, or make a donation to the Red Cross, whose helpers all across Europe were mentioned by some of the refugees I spoke to during my research.

If you or your school raise money or collect goods for these or other refugee charities, email me via the 'email Cathy' link on my website *www.cathycassidy.com* to tell me what you're doing. You can reach out a hand of friendship to kids like Sami, and show them that we care.

Thank you,
Cathy xxx

Read on for an extract from

Love from Lexie

The little girl is curled up on a second-hand sofa, snuggled in a handmade rainbow-striped jumper, her dark hair braided with bright cotton threads, an upturned library book at her feet. She is alone, hugging a knitted toy dog and watching *Frozen*.

Sometimes she pads into the kitchen to look at the clock on the wall. Sometimes she goes to the window and presses her cheek against the glass, looking up at the clear blue sky and then down to the pavement ten floors below.

She peels back the foil from a half-eaten Easter egg and nibbles it absently. When the movie finishes she goes to check the clock once more, then returns to the window. The pavement glitters with broken glass and broken dreams, and when her eyes blur with tears she wipes them fiercely away with her sleeve.

She stays there, watching, waiting, until it gets dark.

1

How It All Began

Have you ever been lost? I have.

In a supermarket when I was a toddler; at a funfair, briefly, aged four or five; on a day trip to Glasgow when I was seven, in the crowds on Buchanan Street. Each time, I was scared, panicked. Each time, my mum found me, wiped my tears, hugged me tight, took my hand and made it all better.

I thought that was just the way things were, the way things always would be. If you were lost, your mum would find you and make things better. I took it for granted.

I didn't realize back then that not everything that gets lost can be found again.

*

I was nine years old when it happened, and I wish I could say I'd seen it coming, but I really didn't . . . I didn't have a clue. For starters, we didn't live a regular kind of life. We moved around a lot.

For a while we lived in a flat in Edinburgh, then a farmhouse in the Scottish borders, a cottage by the sea, and once, for a whole summer, in a bell tent.

We ended up in a high-rise block of flats on a Midlands estate, which was probably the worst place of all . . . but we were happy. Well, I thought we were.

The lifts smelled of sick and the pavements were starred with broken glass, but at last we had a proper flat with a TV and everything. There was no garden, but Mum said the sky belonged to us. We were on the tenth floor, so there was plenty of it.

'We could spread our wings and fly, Lexie,' she told me a few months after we moved in. 'Go anywhere! London, Brighton, the south of France . . . You pick!'

'We could stay here,' I said uncertainly, but Mum said that was boring. She took my hands and danced me around the flat, laughing, but after a while I pulled away, pressed my nose against the windowpane and watched my breath blur and mist the glass. It was the Easter break and the sky was unexpectedly blue, spread out before me like a promise. I was weary of the moves by then, weary of endless new starts in new schools with new best friends who were never going to be forever friends.

'I'm not a staying-in-one-place kind of person!' Mum said.

'I think I might be,' I told her.

She ruffled my hair and told me not to be so silly, but she seemed anxious, doubtful. 'There's a whole wide world out there to explore,' she said, as if trying to convince herself. 'We'll get out there, the two of us, find new adventures! We'll find ourselves!'

I frowned. 'But . . . we're not lost,' I said.

'We are, Lexie,' Mum replied, and her eyes went all sad and faraway. 'We are.'

The next day Mum had an interview in town.

'I won't be too long,' she told me. 'A few hours at most – I might pop to the shops on my way back. You can watch a DVD while I'm gone.'

I slid *Frozen* into the DVD player and snuggled up on the sofa while Mum scribbled a shopping list on the back of an envelope. *Bread, milk, chocolate spread*, it said.

'I'll be back before it's finished,' she said, nodding towards the TV, and I barely looked up, just waved, my eyes still on the screen.

Mum went out just after 2 p.m. and she didn't come back.

Nina Lawlor,
Flat 7/10
S

♥ ♥

Dear Mum,

I waited as long as I could, but they came to

get me in the end. I am staying with a foster

family now but there are too many kids and

I don't really like it. It is on Kenilworth Road but

I forget the number because it fell off the door.

I am at a different school, the one near the

park. Please come and find me soon. I miss you

to the moon and back.

Love,

Lexie xxx

Cathy Cassidy

the chocolate box series

Cherry:
Dark almond eyes. skin the colour of milky coffee, wild imagination, feisty, fun . . .

Skye:
Wavy blonde hair, blue eyes, smiley, individual, kind . . .

Summer:
Slim, graceful, pretty, loves to dance, determined, a girl with big dreams . . .

Coco:
Blue eyes, fair hair, freckles, a tomboy who loves animals and wants to change the world . . .

Honey:
Willowy, blonde, beautiful, arty and out of control, a rebel . . .

Jake:
Jake is about to discover that you can't outrun destiny . . .